Here was her husband-to-be.

Lana grabbed the rail for support as she nearly tripped down the last stair.

It seemed as if the entire hotel staff and guests had turned out for the occasion—the parlor was filled with peering eyes. Lana felt very much on display, even here among strangers. Mack was right—she'd never have survived this charade in the middle of Treasure Creek.

"You're a fine sight," he said as she stepped onto the parlor rug. His voice was tight and unsteady.

"You cut a fine figure yourself," she managed, then gulped at how foolish the words sounded. He really had surprised her, however. In all the muddy making-do of Treasure Creek, she'd completely forgotten the way he could command a room when formally dressed. Half her bridesmaids had swooned over him at her wedding. Her first wedding.

Stop that. You can't think about that now. This is a new life.

ALASKAN BRIDES:
Women of the Gold Rush
find that love is the greatest treasure of all.

Yukon Wedding—Allie Pleiter, April 2011
Klondike Medicine Woman—Linda Ford, May 2011
Gold Rush Baby—Dorothy Clark, June 2011

Books by Allie Pleiter

Love Inspired Historical

Masked by Moonlight
Mission of Hope
Yukon Wedding

Love Inspired

My So-Called Love Life
The Perfect Blend
*Bluegrass Hero
*Bluegrass Courtship
*Bluegrass Blessings
*Bluegrass Christmas
Easter Promises
*"Bluegrass Easter"

*Kentucky Corners

Steeple Hill Books

Bad Heiress Day
Queen Esther & the Second Graders of Doom

ALLIE PLEITER

Enthusiastic but slightly untidy mother of two, RITA® Award finalist Allie Pleiter writes both fiction and nonfiction. An avid knitter and unreformed chocoholic, she spends her days writing books, drinking coffee and finding new ways to avoid housework. Allie grew up in Connecticut, holds a B.S. in Speech from Northwestern University and spent fifteen years in the field of professional fundraising. She lives with her husband, children and a Havanese dog named Bella in the suburbs of Chicago, Illinois.

Yukon Wedding

ALLIE PLEITER

Love Inspired

Special thanks and acknowledgment to Allie Pleiter
for her contribution to the Alaskan Brides miniseries.

Recycling programs
for this product may
not exist in your area.

™ LOVE INSPIRED BOOKS

ISBN-13: 978-0-373-82863-0

YUKON WEDDING

Copyright © 2011 by Harlequin Books, S.A.

www.LoveInspiredBooks.com

Printed in U.S.A.

Do not store up for yourselves treasures on earth, where moth and rust destroy, and where thieves break in and steal. But store up for yourselves treasures in heaven, where moth and rust do not destroy, and where thieves do not break in and steal. For where your treasure is, there your heart will be also.

—*Matthew* 6:18–21

To everyone—and I mean everyone—
at Comer Children's Hospital at the University of Chicago

Chapter One

Treasure Creek, Alaska, June 1898

Mack Tanner looked up to see a raging storm coming toward him.

"Good morning," said the storm, otherwise known as Lana Bristow. Each syllable of her greeting was sharp and steely. She stood in that particular way he called her "speechifying" stance, which heralded an oncoming verbal assault. Mack spread his own feet, not particularly eager to endure whatever was coming in front of the half dozen gold rush stampeders he'd managed to hire off the Chilkoot Trail to build his new General Store.

Lana's blond hair was a nest of frayed locks, strands sticking wildly out of the careful twist she usually wore. Her apron hung diagonally across that impossibly tiny waist of hers, with a wide smear of something dark that matched the smudge currently gracing her son Georgie's chin. The brooch she always wore at her neck—that silly, frilly flower thing with all the golden swirls on it—was gone. It was held bent and misshapen, he noticed with a gulp, in her left hand, while she clamped two-year-old Georgie to one hip with her right. One side of her hem was soaked and the boy sported only one shoe.

More was amiss than the argument he'd had with her last night, that was certain. They'd gone at it again regarding Lana's accounts. Her mounting debts had been a constant sore spot between them since her husband, Jed—Mack's best friend—had died in the Palm Sunday avalanche. She'd caught him monkeying with her store credit again, giving her more than what she paid for and "misplacing" numerous bills. And yes, Mack had taken it upon himself to slash her debt so that no one in Treasure Creek would guess the sorry state of her finances.

He owed her that much.

She didn't see it that way.

Instead, his "generosity" made her furious. Why that confounding woman wouldn't let him settle things up for her—when she needed it and he had the resources to easily do so—never ceased to amaze him.

Lana stood stiff and tall. "I have something to say."

Mack could have been blind, deaf, half asleep and *still* have picked up on that. Every inch of her body broadcast "I have something to say." A low commentary grumble to that effect rippled through the men around him until Mack raised his hand— the one with the large hammer still in it—to silence them.

Not taking his eyes off her, Mack shifted his weight and nodded slowly. For a moment he considered motioning her toward a less public place, seeing as this was no doubt going to be a long "something to say," but the flash of fire in her blue eyes told him to stay put. He had the odd sensation of facing a firing squad.

"Yes." That single syllable loudly declared, Lana spun on her heels, hoisted her son farther up on one hip, and started back down the way she came.

Mack's mouth fell open, letting the nails tumble out to jingle on the ground at his feet. *Yes?* What kind of riddle thing was that to say? Glory, but the Widow Bristow would be the death of him.

The men found this hilarious, sputtering into laughter and less-than-polite commentary until he threw down the hammer and strode off after her. Once away from the crowd, Mack expected Lana to turn and explain herself. It's what rational people did, after all. When after twenty paces she failed to either turn or slow, he bellowed, "Yes what?" after her. It echoed across the intersection, raising heads on either side of the roads that made up the center of tiny Treasure Creek.

Lana stopped and whipped around to face him. The sudden move forced Georgie to grab at her just to stay upright, balling the neckline of her blouse in his toddler fists. Lana glared at Mack as if he must be dimwitted not to catch her meaning. "I said, *'Yes what?'*" he shouted again, not caring which of the curious onlookers gathered on the boardwalks heard him.

Lana furrowed her brows so far down she looked catlike. She flicked her eyes around at the small crowd now staring at them, as if his simple request for a reasonable explanation was some sort of cruel punishment. Lana took three steps toward him, and with something more like a hiss than a whisper, said, "For the *seventh* time, yes." Having spoken her piece, she turned once again and set off up the boardwalk away from him.

Mack slapped his hat against his thigh, confused and angry. What was that supposed to mean, "the seventh time"? What had he done six times that this now was the seventh...

It struck him like a bolt of lightening, thundering though his chest as if struck by the hammer he'd held moments ago.

She'd said "yes."

As in "Yes, I will marry you."

He'd asked her six times over the last two months, the first time only a week after her Jed's tragic death. Marrying her was the best way to protect her now. After all, he'd lured Jed up here with the promise of fortune and adventure. A promise that ended with Jed buried in snow, alongside dozens of other stampeders who refused to heed their guide's warnings that Sunday. He could have done more to stop Jed, to make his foolhardy buddy see reason and be cautious. But he hadn't, and now Lana was left up here on her own—without Jed and without the fortune he'd made and subsequently lost.

He'd asked her over and over after that, even though she blamed him for Jed's death, knowing she'd rather marry a log than wed the likes of him, well aware of how much she disliked him, but equally aware that it was the only real way to make it up to her and her son. He'd asked her every time she struggled with this thing or that, every time she'd looked weary from keeping up appearances. He asked every time it looked as if the endless struggles of Alaskan living—and the greedy stream of despicable Alaskan men—were about to do her in.

Once, when a drunken "old friend of Jed's" had actually tried to drag her off to Skaguay and marry her by force, he'd even offered to pay her way back to Seattle. She had no family left back there, but he was plumb out of ways to keep her safe when too many stampeders still thought she held Jed's riches. After all, he'd known Jed's lust for gold was growing beyond reason and into desperation. He could have tried harder to protect Jed from the impulsive nature that was always his undoing. The fact that Jed was gone was his fault.

She knew he could have tried harder to save Jed, too. She'd refused every single offer of help.

Until now.

So why was his now new fiancée stomping off without an explanation? He'd lived long enough to know that a female could be the most furious of God's creations when provoked, but he would *not* allow her to stomp off with the last word.

Especially when that last word was "yes."

Grumbling that his keen sense of obligation would likely be the death of him, Mack set off after her. She stalked past the white church—one of the first buildings he and Jed had built when they founded the town—and still didn't look back. Georgie did, though, catching Mack's gaze with troubled brown eyes under that mop of curly dark hair. His mama kept up her furious pace, past the other shops and houses, attracting the stares of the men gathered along the boardwalk. She and Georgie were sulking off to her cabin, from the looks of it. She had to know he'd follow her, even if she kept her back ramrod straight as she turned the corner past the schoolhouse.

The Tucker sisters, a trio of rough-and-tumble gals who'd spent the past month working on that building, stopped their work to look up at the spectacle. Lucy Tucker waved, but Lana stomped on, paying Lucy no mind. Buildings sprung up overnight like mushrooms here in Treasure Creek. Mack felt on display as the sisters gawked among themselves. With his town nearing a thousand residents and ten times that many rushing through in a steady stream toward the Trail, why did all them have time this morning to watch Mack Tanner make a fool of himself?

Lana didn't think she had any tears left to cry. She made her way back through the crowded, muddy main street, past the church Mack and Jed had insisted mark the center of the town they'd founded together just three months ago. Three months that felt like thirty years. She picked her way as fast as she could past the schoolhouse under construction, the bank and several rows of cobbled together shacks where farmers and butchers sold food. She didn't stop until she reached the cabin she and Georgie called home. She hadn't expected to cry, couldn't believe that tears threatened now, and would not, absolutely *would not* cry in public.

Mack was behind her, she knew it. And he ought to be, if he had an ounce of compassion in that stubborn, domineering head of his. She was sure she heard the thud of his angry boots behind her as she rounded the corner beyond Mavis Goodge's boardinghouse, but she wouldn't give him the satisfaction of letting him see her turn.

She'd done it. She'd surrendered to the only viable option available to her in Treasure Creek. Some "treasure." It was awful here—cold and crude, muddy and noisy—and this was one of the *better* towns. It seemed ages ago when Mack and Jed had founded Treasure Creek. They'd been full of big ideas, seeking to create a place of faith and values in the lawless, greedy chaos of the gold rush. Only it hadn't turned out that way. Not for her. Yes, Treasure Creek had become known as a God-fearing town, but what good had faith done in the face of all the rampant swindling of the Chilkoot Trail? Faith hadn't kept Jed off the trail that Sunday, even though the guides warned "the mountain was angry." Faith hadn't squelched Jed's relentless need to chase gold rumors, skipping Sunday services to meet an Indian guide boasting leads to an undiscovered lode. God hid no huge, undiscovered treasures up on that mountain. In her darker moments, Lana believed God sent the deadly wall of snow, stranding her up here and stealing Georgie's father. A vengeful God punished her husband's greed, backing her into so dark a corner that she must accept a marriage of convenience to Mack Tanner.

She laughed at the thought as she pushed open the door of her cabin and stepped into the tiny confines. It wasn't a marriage of convenience. It was a marriage of *survival*. And survive she would. Here, because here seemed to be the only place there was.

It had struck her last night, after yet another argument over her accounts with Mack, just how bad things had gotten. The point had been pushed home, literally, when she snatched her favorite brooch out of Georgie's hand and pricked herself on the now-bent pinpoint. The toddler had gotten into her jewelry box when she'd left it open after sorting through which jewels she might be able to sell discreetly in Skaguay. Some jewelry box. The rustic chest Jed had built her on her last birthday could barely be called such a thing. Life here was nowhere near what she dreamed it would be. She ought to be thankful that Georgie hadn't speared himself with the brooch before she found him. As it was, Georgie had managed to bend and dent the soft gold by banging it against the hearth until its floral shape was lost forever.

Why did she wear a brooch out here in the first place? Purely ornamental, it wasn't strong enough to hold a shawl or cloak together and it snagged on everything. Still, she wore it daily, a flag of refined defiance. No one would ever know how badly Jed had left their finances. She was and always would be "a lady of means."

Trouble was, she had precious little means left. Lana had realized, as she stared at the broken brooch, that her former self—the delicate Seattle socialite who'd followed her husband on his grand fortune hunt—no longer existed. She couldn't limp back to Seattle and be some man's useless ornament. She craved independence now, but it was a hollow craving without sufficient means.

Women could achieve astounding independence up here. The concept of "female" had been reinvented in Alaska. Transformed into something she wanted very much to be. She couldn't bring herself to turn from that freedom now. Not only that, but to sulk back to Seattle would be to admit that Jed and his adventures had all been nothing more than smoke and mirrors. Lana refused to count herself among the thousands of duped and squandered fortune hunters. Treasure Creek, for all the pain it held, was still the lesser of all available evils. Seattle might be more comfortable, and there were things Georgie could have there that she could never give him here, but Lana had swallowed so much pride over the past three months that she didn't think she could stomach the feast of humility it would take to head south.

I'll do whatever it takes to stay here, she told herself as she pulled the cabin door shut behind her with a declarative slam. *Whatever it takes.*

She turned and looked at Mack through the cabin's only window. Even if it takes *him.* The tears she'd held in finally burst out in sobs so great they shook Georgie as he clung to her side.

He stood perhaps a hundred paces from her home, staring at her closed door. The patient, dark expression on his face mirrored the way he looked that awful night Jed died. She'd cursed him that night two months ago, cursed their plans to carve a wholesome community out of the greedy scramble that Alaska had become. She'd gone so far as to accuse Mack of urging Jed on too far, of leading Jed to his death as if he'd sent the avalanche himself.

Mack had stood there then, dark and silent as he was now, letting her call all sorts of guilt down on his head, without a single word of dispute. Mack hadn't killed Jed; Jed's own greed led him to his death, driving him to the point where he ignored the Indian guide's advice to stay off the trail that Sunday. He seemed to accept her hate as his penance for not keeping Jed from his foolish self.

She hated the thought that his repeated proposals were just more of the same penance—obligation rather than affection. Affection would have followed her into the cabin, swept her off her feet with some dashing kiss and spun her around the room like the world's finest prize, the way Jed had done.

As it was, obligation stood in her front yard, angry but immovably resolved, like some sort of monument to their mutual resignation.

Mercy, Lana, she lectured herself in her mother's voice, *you can't hate him like this. It's no way to start.*

Lana wiped her eyes. Alaskan women never admitted defeat. Alaskan women figured out how to carve a life from the harsh realities around them. If she wanted to be an Alaskan woman she needed to steel herself and face facts. And the fact was Mack Tanner was her only option if Georgie was to have a decent home and father.

Stepping into a future she hoped was worth her present pain, Lana pulled open the cabin door. "You'd best come inside and settle things."

Chapter Two

Mack couldn't even believe he had to ask. "Why did you finally agree to my proposal?"

Lana looked surprised, as if it was obvious. Why were women always so impossible? Why would something so cryptic as why one proposal gets accepted when the previous six were declined be *obvious?*

She broke a biscuit in half and handed it to Georgie as he sat on the rug. For the hundredth time Mack looked into the tot's dark eyes and saw Jed's face stare back at him.

"Would you like me to say it was your irresistible charm?"

Glory, she was infuriating. "I think I'm entitled to the truth, don't you?"

"Truth. Oh, that's an ideal to be sure. We've got far too much of it up here, and loads more deception besides, wouldn't you say?"

Odd as the paradox was, Lana had a point. Alaska overflowed with deceived folks slamming up against the harshness of truth. It was part of the reason he'd come here with Jed, to build a town that gave folks the truth about surviving the Chilkoot Trail. Treasure Creek had no saloons and no swindlers, only good, honest folk bent on equipping stampeders for the very real dangers ahead.

They'd founded Treasure Creek with a single building—the church, as a matter of principle—but God had blessed their efforts and Treasure Creek was growing almost faster than anyone could manage. Every man they convinced to leave off the foolhardy pursuits of the gold digging was a victory to Mack. Every ill-prepared or deceived man who died up there seemed a tragic, preventable loss.

Losses like Jed. "Why?" he repeated, more softly this time. She'd clearly been up all night and crying besides, so it can't have been an easy decision. She deserved whatever tenderness his baffled surprise could muster.

Lana straightened her spine, resolve settling her expression into a quiet he'd not seen on her before. "There wasn't another way," she said matter-of-factly.

He'd known that all along. Spirited as she was, Lana wasn't made of strong enough stock to go it alone. Nevertheless, it jarred him to hear her put it so bluntly. He didn't know what he expected from the moment, but it wasn't this. Her answer was more surrender than agreement. It wasn't as though he expected enthusiasm, but her tone couldn't help but confirm marriage to him was a last-chance proposition.

Mack stuffed his hands in his pockets. "I was thinking it might be best if we went off to Skaguay to marry. Day after tomorrow. Skip trying to do the wedding here and just keep it private. I've got some business in town anyways," he added, afraid to admit he was doing it mostly for her sake. "So I thought maybe the Tucker sisters would take Georgie for a day or two. You could do some shopping while you're there. Things for the house and all."

Suddenly it felt brazen to refer to the fact that she'd be moving in. Which was nonsense—of course she'd be moving in—but it just opened up a whole, wriggly issue of what kind of marriage he had in mind. He'd been clear about it before: he was offering his protection without expecting anything—*anything* in return. She just never seemed to believe him. The air in the cabin grew hot and prickly, and he looked around the room in the gap of silence. It was one of Treasure Creek's nicer cabins—he and Jed had seen to that—but nice by Treasure Creek standards was a far cry from what he knew Lana was used to. What Lana had wanted.

In what Jed had always referred to as "the high times," the Bristow place was lush and showy. Now, despite how little she had, Lana still managed to add fancy touches. The crude table in her cabin always had a tablecloth, even if it was cut from an old skirt. She always carried a handkerchief everywhere she went. He thought it ridiculous when she'd sewn a ruffle to the oilcloth that covered the cabin window to make it look more like a curtain. Now he couldn't picture her windows without it.

"There'll be no…expectations," he reassured her again, feeling ridiculously awkward. "Our arrangement is purely for your protection. And Georgie's."

Lana took forever to answer. And even before she did, she gestured for him to sit down at the table, then arranged herself carefully opposite him. She smoothed the worn little tablecloth out with her hands. "I suppose Skaguay would be a good idea."

"Still, I want you to know I intend to do this up right." He'd buy her a fine wedding dress, good meals and they'd stay in a nice hotel far from the seedy side of town. Of course, Skaguay didn't really have a nice part—the entire city was a wild, lawless den of thieves—but it was also one of the few places nearby where things of any civility could be had. Refinements were important to Lana, and he owed her that much.

Mack also knew, without her saying it, that a town-wide, smiling-faced wedding in Treasure

Creek would be more than she could bear. This marriage was raw, difficult territory for both of them. A little privacy was the only decent thing to do under the circumstances. That, and the very practical consideration that there wasn't anyone capable of legally marrying them in Treasure Creek. Mack knew the town needed a preacher, but now Mack *personally* needed to ensure that more than his impassioned but unordained preaching filled the pulpit at Treasure Creek Christian Church. "We can have a fine meal and some new clothes. Get some nice things," he repeated, getting back to the subject at hand. "For you. For Georgie."

Her eyes narrowed. "I've made my decision, Mack. There's no need to lure me in."

She made it sound like he'd won some kind of standoff. Trapped her like prize game. That's not how this was, and she knew it. "I'm a gentleman, Lana. One who knows how a wife ought to be treated, and of no mind to skip that on account of… odd circumstances. We don't need a big shindig, but nothing says we can't make the best of things. My wife will have nice things." It came out like a command rather than the statement of value he'd intended it.

"Out here?" She looked at the sad little jelly jar of wildflowers that sat on her frayed tablecloth as if it were evidence of how "nice" Treasure Creek was.

"Yes, even *out here*," he said sharply, mostly to

defy the infuriating look in her eye. It was a sorry
retort, but she had a gift for driving him to that.
"And Georgie, too. He'll be provided for. You both
will." He'd promised Jed and Lana a bright future,
and he was going to make that future possible, even
if it made his present miserable.

It took exactly two hours for word to get out. By
the time Lana arrived at the home of the Tucker sisters, a trio of spinsters who held marriage—and men
in general—in low esteem, it was obvious they'd
already heard the news. Frankie, the oldest and
arguably the prickliest of the trio, planted her hands
on her hips the moment Lana stepped in their door.
"Well, now I know why you was in such a huff earlier. Mack, huh? I suppose if you felt you had to go
and marry someone…" She made it sound like even
worse of a necessary evil than it was. While Lana
admired their spunk—and coming from somewhere
in Oklahoma, they had spunk and drawls to spare—
they were far too rough for her liking. They'd come
to Treasure Creek not long after she and Jed, but
more for the adventure of a free life than any greed
for gold. More like lumberjacks than any of Seattle's
society ladies, the Tuckers spent their days building
the town's tiny almost-up-and-running schoolhouse.
They may have built the school, but Lana found
them the furthest thing from "schoolmarms" she
could imagine.

Not that they weren't friendly; they were kind and bighearted as the day was long, but "rough around the edges" was putting it mildly. Of course, Georgie loved the shocking, free-wheeling trio, and they adored him. Even though some part of her brain worried that the sisters' appetite for mischief outpaced even Georgie's, Mack had been smart in his idea to ask them to watch the toddler. They'd accept in a heartbeat, and Treasure Creek wasn't boasting a whole lot of families able to take in a toddler on short notice. Besides, three-on-one was barely fair odds when it came to Georgie.

Once inside, Georgie headed straight for the "cookie jar" the sisters kept on their table. The Tuckers often gave Georgie what they believed passed for "cookies." Lana thought they were closer to sailor's hardtack than anything that would pass in Seattle for a cookie. That hardly mattered to Georgie; he gladly accepted every one they doled out.

"Mack is a fine man," Lana said, defending him to the now glowering Frankie, as the small, wiry woman reached into the cookie jar. Frankie replied by shaking her head and making a derisive snort as she plunked a dense beige circle into Georgie's chubby palm.

"Well, I suppose he is," Frankie's sister Margie conceded as she stood against the mantel and stuffed her hands into the pockets of the odd split skirt she wore tucked into huge black boots. "But that don't mean you have to *marry* him. Not up here."

Most especially up here, Lana thought. She'd been so taken up with making the painful decision, she hadn't had time to think about the fact that other people would actually have to know. *How ridiculous,* she chastised herself as she felt her cheeks flush, *of course everyone will know.* Mack had been kind enough to keep his relentless marital campaign a secret, so she hadn't had to deal with the public consequences of becoming Mrs. Mack Tanner until this moment. It made her feel foolish to be blindsided by something so obvious.

Lucy, the youngest of the trio, came in from the other room scratching her short dark hair. Lana had the unkind thought that that was probably the closest that her hair ever came to being brushed. Lucy had a gift for getting under Lana's skin, far more than the other two. Perhaps it was her age as the youngest, but it might also be the lovely woman Lana expected Lucy might really be under all that bawdy demeanor. "I guess we'll have us a wedding! That'll be fun." She turned to her sisters. "We ever had a wedding in Treasure Creek before?"

Margie twisted her mouth up in thought. "Can't recall one. Should be a hoot!"

"Well actually, that's what I came to talk to you about. I was hoping you could watch Georgie while Mack and I go into Skaguay to make it official."

"Skaguay?" Lucy balked. "You're not marrying here? Mack built that church. First off even, practically before he built his own home. Why, he and Jed…" Her voice trailed off as she realized why marrying Mack in the church Jed helped build might pose a problem. Lana began to wonder if this could get more awkward. "Still, you'd think…"

Lana didn't want to get into this with anyone, much less the Tuckers. "We haven't got a real preacher here to do it, Lucy. And we need to buy things for the house." It irked her that she'd had to resort to Mack's reasoning—or was it Mack's excuses?—but she was stumped for a better answer. "He wants us to have a fancy time of it. You know, as a gift and all."

The sisters all raised eyebrows, clearly showing what they thought of that idea.

"It's the only place we can order books and such for the school, too. I walked past the schoolhouse this morning. It's nearly done, thanks to you." Lana hoped the compliment would divert their attentions.

Nothing doing. "Oh, we saw you *walk* past the schoolhouse," Frankie cackled. "Lovebirds, the pair of you."

This was going to be harder than Lana thought. "Can you watch him?" she asked, in the sweetest version of her *we're not going to have that conversation voice.*

Lucy bent down and ruffled Georgie's hair, something that always bothered Lana but sent Georgie into fits of giggles. "Of course we can watch the little fellow. Think of it as a wedding present. A little privacy for the happy couple, hmm?"

Her bawdy tone sent the trio into laughter, elbowing each other like a crowd of sailors. Worse yet, Georgie laughed right along with them. Lana began to wonder if the next boat back to Seattle might not be so horrible after all.

Chapter Three

As it was, the next boat Lana boarded was the ferry to Skaguay, beside her soon-to-be husband. While difficult to endure, the short burst of congratulations from everyone in Treasure Creek only proved Mack's insight correct—this really was best done out of town.

And as Mack had declared, best done right. *If one can't have a nice marriage, one can at least have a nice wedding,* Lana thought to herself as she admired her fetching new dress in the big mirror of her hotel room. It was so elegant a thing, for being done on such short notice. A smart lavender shirtwaist with just enough ruffle to make it fussy skimmed over a tiered skirt of the same pale hue. As a widow, she needn't bother with either train or veil, so she'd get to wear the dress again for formal occasions back in Treasure Creek.

The phrase made her laugh. Formal occasions didn't really happen back in Treasure Creek. Folks were too busy surviving to think of such things. Still, if Mack was "Mr. Treasure Creek," as the Tucker sisters jokingly called him, then that meant she was about to become Mrs. Treasure Creek. It was too long since she'd thought of any "social" event. How wonderful it would be to create a town festival or a church social. Surely she could find time in the nearly twenty hours of daylight Alaskan summer days brought.

They'd spent the full day yesterday buying things. Cloth and linens, not just one but three new table-cloths and curtains—real curtains, not just make-do ones like she had back in her cabin. New shoes and pants for Georgie, and a little wooden train set Mack had picked out himself. And books. Nearly a dozen books sat in the corner of her hotel room now. Two novels, two cookery books and a whole set of sample schoolbooks Mack had ordered crates of for the schoolhouse back home. The real surprise had come when she'd stopped to admire a pair of pearl earrings in a store window and Mack had taken her inside and bought them for her. Then he'd deposited her at a dressmaker's while he went off to do "some business," telling her to get any dress she wanted to wear today. And any shoes and any hat to match.

Lana Bristow, you are too easily bought, she chided herself, her thoughts snagging on the truth that she would only bear that name for perhaps another hour, if that. Of course, she could never let Mack see how easily her head had been turned by a trinket here and a new dress there, but it had been ages since she'd had a hot, scented bath like she'd had this morning.

Mrs. Smithton, proprietress of the mostly quiet, mostly respectable Smithton's Shining Harbor Hotel, came into the room again. Skaguay didn't see many weddings, and Mrs. Smithton had joyously intruded into all the proceedings. So much so that even Lana, who usually loved being fussed over, was reaching the end of her patience.

She could only imagine the state of Mack's nerves under such enthusiastic scrutiny. After all, she had been through this before. Mack had never been a groom. She flinched at the still-absurd thought that she was going to marry Mack Turner. In a matter of minutes.

Lana blanched and clenched her fists. "Oh, dearie," said Mrs. Smithton, "every bride gets the fits just before. Never you worry. You've kept one glove off, like I told you?" Lana found Mrs. Smithton's concern over "good luck" wedding traditions ironic. Mack never believed in "luck," and given all the tragedy they'd been though, the thought of her marriage being endangered by looking into the mirror fully dressed seemed silly.

The round older woman fussed with the netting on the smart, feathered hat that sat on Lana's piled-high hair. "Besides," Mrs. Smithton whispered with a wink, "he's a far sight worse off'n you, if you ask me. Looks as pale as a fish, he does. Fright looks funny on a big feller like him. Been up since dawn and barely eaten a thing."

So he *was* nervous. Even in his fluster, Mack had seen to it that tea, toast and peach jam—her very favorite—were sent up this morning. He seemed to know so many little things about her, and yet she still felt like, even after several years, she'd barely paid enough attention to know the color of his eyes. They were blue, weren't they? She knew so little of him.

He'd been clear on the type of marriage he proposed. Even yesterday he had assured her theirs would be an arrangement of "mutual convenience," not "emotional entanglements." Still, tangle was as close to describing whatever it was she felt toward Mack Tanner. It no longer mattered, did it? This had never been about sentiment, only survival. Lana shut her eyes tight. Too late to worry about the consequences of survival now. *Whatever it takes,* she told herself. *He's not a horrible man.*

She said it over and over to herself silently, as Mrs. Smithton led her down the hall to stand at the top of the stairs and view her groom. *He's not a horrible man.*

Mack's eyes were indeed blue. Very, very blue. They stared up at her as she came down the hotel stairs, a fair bit of panic showing in their depths. Decidedly un-horrible, Mack looked elegant in a dark suit and a gray vest. The black tie knotted under his starched white collar made the blue of his eyes stand out all the more. His hair, mostly a tumultuous mass of unruly dark waves, had been neatly slicked back in the style of the day. She had the odd thought that she hadn't seen him so clean in months, and the equally odd thought that it suited him. He looked exactly like the well-to-do man she remembered from their Seattle days. This Mack Tanner was as much the man Jed admired as Mack Tanner the rugged adventurer.

Mack Tanner her husband-to-be. Lana grabbed the rail for support as she nearly tripped down the last stair.

It seemed as if the entire hotel staff and guests had turned out for the occasion—the parlor was filled with peering eyes. Men elbowed each other, making whispered remarks about the "poor feller" while the room's few women oohed and ahhed. Lana felt very much on display, even here among strangers. Mack was right—she'd never have survived this charade if this were Mavis Goodge's boardinghouse in the middle of Treasure Creek.

"You're a fine sight," he said as she stepped onto the parlor rug. His voice was tight and unsteady.

"You cut a fine figure yourself," she managed, then gulped at how foolish the words sounded. He really had surprised her, however. In all the muddy making-do of Treasure Creek, she'd completely forgotten the way he could command a room when formally dressed. Half her bridesmaids had swooned over him at her wedding. Her *first* wedding.

Stop that. You can't think about that now. This is a new life. That old Lana is long gone.

Lana made herself smile as Mack tipped his hat to Mrs. Smithton and held out an elbow. "If you don't mind, Mrs. Smithton, we've an appointment to keep."

Lana's stomach tumbled like a windstorm as they walked down the street. The Good Lord had never seen a wedding day like this, she was sure. It didn't really matter, she supposed, what the Good Lord thought of this whole business. He'd pretty much left her on her own, as far as she was concerned.

Mack wouldn't take to such thinking. It was easy to see the strength of that man's faith. Even in the darkest of times, faith was like a constant compass for him. The man had built the town's church before his own dwelling had solid walls. He preached on Sundays, doing an admirable job filling in, until someone took the pulpit permanently. Jed had admired that, too.

She'd lost any sense of that "true north" compass needle of faith, her inner compass spinning aimlessly since the day the avalanche took Jed. Her husband's spirituality had been mostly sputtering sparks of faith fed by Mack's constant flame. Intense but inconsistent. Jed aspired to, but never quite achieved, a lot of Mack's traits. *Stop comparing them. Stop it.*

"You all right?" Mack's voice was saying. He'd

stilled and she hadn't even noticed. "You look a bit—"

"Well, so do you!" she shot back, not wanting him to finish that sentence, then bit her lip. The man was simply trying to be nice, and here she was, biting his head off.

Mack gave out a nervous laugh. "Well, good to see you've still got some fight in you. And here I thought maybe I'd left the old Lana back on the dock at Treasure Creek." He pushed out a breath, closing his eyes for a second or two. "It'll be all right," he said quietly when he opened them again. "It'll be… just fine."

"Of course it will," she lied emphatically. He knew it, too. Without a word of retort, Mack merely crinkled up the corner of his eyes and tucked her hand deeper into the crook of his arm, and they walked on.

"That's a fine dress. Look at the way folks are staring at us," he said, keeping a tight grip on her arm. Whether the gesture was meant to be reassuring or constraining, she couldn't say. "You always did like to be the center of attention. I'd say you've got it here, surely."

"*I* like being the center of attention? This from the man who makes himself the center of Treasure Creek? We *are* a pair, you and I." She could almost chuckle about that, and it made her feel just a bit better.

"'Course, I will be insisting on the 'obey' part in

our vows, you know," he said, a laugh now tickling the edges of his deep voice. "Just to be clear on things."

"If you're fixing to get obeyed, then I'm fixing to get honored. You know, just to be clear on things."

He looked at her with that. "Well then, I guess we really are a pair."

It wasn't much of a ceremony. The pastor's wife stood in as witness, and despite the Bible and the prayers, the whole thing had an efficient, stamp of approval feel. Treasure Creek's makeshift dockmaster, Caleb Johnson, might have been signing off on a daily shipment, for all the ceremony's sentiment. Still, her heart did a funny jump when Mack looked her square in the eye as he pledged to honor and cherish her. It wasn't a romantic or smitten look, but the strong sense of honor struck her hard. She knew, as he looked at her, held her hand with a steady grip and slipped a new and different ring on the fourth finger of her left hand, that he *would* honor her.

Lana wasn't prepared for what that would do to her. She hadn't realized, until his vow, how deeply alone she'd felt. The crushing black knot in her chest loosened with his words. Even if she had nothing else, she now had protection. The yawning gap of her own vulnerability—the dark force she'd fought so fiercely every moment since Jed's death, swallowed her and stole her voice, so that her own vows were barely above a tearful whisper. She hadn't cried at her first wedding, but now tears slipped down one cheek as the minister smiled and pronounced them man and wife.

It was done. And somehow, it had not been the earth-shattering moment she feared. It was a passage. A quiet, gigantic leap from one life into another.

Chapter Four

All through the fancy dinner following the wedding, Mack stared at Lana. Lana Tanner. His wife. He'd arranged for them to spend tonight in Skaguay for her sake, he thought. Now he began to think it was *he* who needed the extra time away from Treasure Creek to get used to his new marital status. The thought still stunned him.

She was a stunning woman. She'd always been beautiful—"a looker" was Jed's favorite term—one best showed off by finery and elegance. The kind of woman a man could dress up and take out on the town with pride. Jed had admitted to him once how astonished he'd been that Lana chose him over Mack. Jed was such a romantic charmer, however, that it hadn't surprised Mack at all that his best friend "got the girl." There'd never been any question in Mack's mind. Lana wasn't his type.

Now Lana was his wife. They were both skittish through every course of the elegant meal, and it had to do with much more than the shadow of their pasts.

He'd already told her—twice—that this was a marriage of arrangement, that there were no expectations of this being anything other than two people living under the same roof. Still, for appearances sake, there could be no question behind which door he slept tonight. Jed was always so much better with women. Mack grimaced at his bumbling awkwardness. He tried to put Jed from his mind and reassure Lana again as he took his bride by the elbow after dinner and led her up the stairs to their honeymoon suite, but it made the moment no less awkward as he slid the lock shut behind them and turned to face the room.

Mrs. Smithton had been regrettably busy. All of Mack's things had been moved into the room. The place was thick with flowers and candles, and a ridiculous amount of petals had been strewn about.

"Oh my," Lana said, her voice nearly a gulp.

"Mrs. Smithton reads too many novels," Mack said, then wished he'd hadn't. Just when he thought this couldn't get more difficult. Lana looked pale. "Lana," he began, moving toward her to catch her if she fainted.

"You haven't changed your mind…have you?"

"Lana…I am not the kind of man to…" Land sakes, how to say this? "To take what…what ought only to be…freely given."

She stilled, her defiance melting into a frailty that took some corner of his heart and ran off with it. "I was afraid once you *could*...you'd want to..."

Now that was just plain cruel. Of course some part of him *wanted*. Any man with blood still running in his veins *wanted*, and she was a beautiful woman.

The irritating, obstinate, distractingly rose-scented widow of his lost friend. He'd better think of something to do, and fast. Out of somewhere in the mists of his jumbled thoughts, he remembered a game his father would play with him when he was sick or in pain. Surely, this was the most absurd use of such a distraction. "How about we talk?"

"Talk?"

"Think of three questions you've always wanted to ask me. The hardest ones you can think of. I promise to give you a truthful answer."

She began pulling off her gloves, eyes scrunched up in thought. Another minute of excruciating silence went by, both of them fidgeting like youngsters. As traces of her usual demeanor returned, she straightened, looked him in the eye and asked, "Are you sorry?"

That was Lana. Always needing to know where she stood, always making sure you knew where you stood with her. Absolutely no mystery with this woman. He gave the question a respectful moment of thought, wanting to word his answer carefully.

"No," he said, sure he meant it. Still, he couldn't resist adding, "not yet."

She managed a small laugh at that, and he was glad to see it. Much of the tension had left the room, and he was glad of that, too. It was late—past ten—and the sun was finally starting its descent behind the mountains. He watched her walk to the window, the fading orb attracting her attention the way it had caught his.

"Mack," she said, her voice soft, "why here? Why in this…"

He knew the term she'd bitten back. She'd used it too many times since Jed's death. "You were going to say 'God-forsaken place,' weren't you?"

She leaned against the window frame, looking like an oil painting in that fancy dress up against the sunset and curtains. "As a matter of fact, I was." She sighed. She tilted her face back to him and added, "Mrs. Mack Turner had better not say such things, hmm?"

Mack leaned against the bedpost, suddenly exhausted. "I've heard worse. But it isn't the talk that bothers me so much as the idea. This place is anything but God-forsaken."

"All those lives. All those people and things lost and broken up on the trail. Jed. Your own brothers, *both* of them. 'God-forsaken' fits, harsh as it is. I just don't see what you see."

Mack walked to the window, still keeping a safe distance from her. In the deepening sunset, the mountains fit the "majestic" description so often employed in the pamphlets enticing men up here. He'd used the word himself when convincing Jed, hadn't he? "They look grand now, from here."

She made a small grunt. "From *here* you can't see all the trash and abandoned equipment and dead horses. Those mountains are still only hungry beasts to me, eager to swallow men up whole."

Mack took a step closer to her, pointed to the peak he knew was closest to Treasure Creek. Its permanent veil of snow gleamed rose-gold in the sunset. "Not all of it. Parts are still clean. Untouched. A fresh start. That's what Treasure Creek was—is— for me. A chance to get a fresh start, to build something solid from the ground up. In a place where there isn't much of that. Remind folks that God didn't forsake one inch of a place like this."

She turned away from the window, looking at him with her head cocked analytically to one side. "Why does a man like you need a fresh start? Seems you've done...fine so far."

"Comes a point in a man's life where he's made money, he's made a name for himself, but he wants to know he's made a difference. Left something better than how he found it."

Lana's laugh had a dark edge. "And you couldn't leave someplace *farther south* better than how you found it?"

"Sometimes you don't choose your challenges. Sometimes your challenges choose you." He suspected he was talking about more than Treasure Creek at the moment.

"I don't know how to do this," she said quietly.

"It's rather easy," he lied, thinking it would be anything but. "You get the bed, I get the floor and we both smile a lot in the morning."

Chapter Five

Mack winced as the ornate clock on his mantel struck eleven the next evening. Georgie, as he had done every hour since arriving at his new home, offered eleven loud "bong!"s in reply.

Lana watched Mack clamp his hand over the little gold chimes and roll his eyes. He was doing his level best to be civil when he inquired, "Does he *ever* sleep?"

Mack's exasperation made her laugh. She'd had that very thought so many times over the past two months, she'd almost come to believe Georgie was incapable of it. Teena Crow, the Tlingit healing woman, had offered her teas to help, but Lana didn't trust those strange native concoctions. As if aware the conversation had turned to him, Georgie walked over and poked Mack in the knee. This brought Mack to squat down to the boy's height and consider Georgie with the narrow-eyed impatience of someone who had their last nerve stomped upon half an hour ago. "It's *bedtime,* George," Mack commanded, pointing up at the clock for emphasis.

"No."

Mack caught Lana's eyes over Georgie's head. *Do something about this,* his expression silently shouted. "Ah, but it is. Your mama knows it is, too."

The great Mack Tanner, flummoxed by a toddler. Were she not so bone-tired herself, she'd have found it amusing. Wound up by all the excitement and the new surroundings of Mack's large cabin, Georgie was about as compliant as a mule. A very cranky, very curious, very irritating little mule. "I do indeed," Lana said, dropping the socks she'd just managed to wrestle off Georgie's feet and dragging herself to the chair by the small fire. Sinking into it, she patted her lap several times. "Come up here and…" She'd meant to ask Mack to bring her one of the children's readers from the stack of books they'd purchased, but the question suddenly raised the issue of what to call Mack now.

"Ugle Ack," Georgie barked pointing in Mack's direction.

"Uncle Mack," Mack replied, sensing not only her unspoken question, but Georgie's unsolicited pronouncement. Mack was Georgie's godfather, and Jed had referred to Mack always as "Uncle Mack" to the boy. For months Georgie could only manage "Ack," which was amusing enough in itself, but over the Christmas holidays he'd graduated to "Ugle Ack."

Perhaps their new marital status was no reason to change that.

"*Uncle Mack* can bring us one of those pretty books with the pictures in them. Mama will read to you."

Mack instantly delivered the book in question. "And Uncle Mack will take a walk," he declared, "to let *things* settle down."

From the moment Caleb Johnson had loudly heralded their arrival on Treasure Creek's dock, Mack, Lana and eventually Georgie been surrounded by an endless stream of well-wishers. Little wonder Georgie was too wound up to sleep, while she could barely hold her eyes open. Lana nodded her approval as she took the book from Mack's outstretched hand. "Bye-bye, Uncle Mack." She used the reader to wave at Mack, fighting a twinge of jealousy at his escape into the quiet night. Georgie babbled a chattering farewell, too, wiggling his fingers while he grabbed at the new diversion.

Mack grumbled something Lana suspected she'd be glad not to have heard, and plucked his hat from its peg by the door. She felt her whole body collapse as the door clicked shut. Alone. She'd been on pins and needles all day, plastering a happy look on her face despite the terrible night's sleep she'd gotten. Mack Tanner snored. Loudly. Still, by the endless sets of shifting she'd heard from his corner of the floor, Lana gathered he'd slept no better, if indeed more loudly. Add one exuberant toddler and everyone was on edge.

"Let's see." She sighed, returning her attention to the fidgety boy in her lap, "what have we got here? *McGuffey's Eclectic Primer.* Uncle Mack knows you need to learn your letters first of all, and look at the pretty pictures!" Georgie, finding this suitable entertainment, settled in against Lana's chest and began sucking on his thumb. Turning to the first page, Lana read, "A is for…ax? Good gracious, who starts off the alphabet with *axes?* I daresay Mr. McGuffey wasn't a papa, if you ask me." She yawned. "A is also for apple, too. You like apples." She'd have a thing or two to say to the esteemed Mr. McGuffey about his opening page if she ever met him. Still, the alphabet continued on with kinder images. Box, cat, dog, elk and so on.

How many nights had Mack walked the town, praying his way though the streets of Treasure Creek, asking God's protection over the people who lived there? It had become his evensong, his nightly ritual, his way of laying to bed the troubles of the day and asking God to send enough wisdom to make it through tomorrow.

It felt different tonight. He could walk through town all he wished, but it would not change the fact that he would go home to a wife and child. Mack had never in his life felt more sure he'd done the right thing, but less certain how to handle the consequences. It might help if his patience weren't strained to the limit by Georgie's boundless energy. The rascal had found six things to break in the first half an hour in his new home.

"Says who?" an angry voice sounded from the side of town where stampeders camped. The constantly shifting tent village housed those waiting their turn up the Chilkoot Trail. Or those limping down off it, thin and hungry. Mack broke up a fight nearly every night. He'd pressed nearly a dozen barely skilled people into stitching up the wounded lately. Even Teena Crow, the healing woman from the local Tlingit tribe, had been forced to double her efforts. Mack wondered how many punches had been thrown—and bones broken—in his time away. These days the medical needs of Treasure Creek threatened to surpass its spiritual needs.

"I'da been rich by now if it ain't for you!" another voice called back. He'd heard every version of this argument under the sun, it seemed. Everyone had someone handy to blame for their failure. Even with Treasure Creek's God-fearing reputation, there were two dozen fools to every successful man. *How do I show them, Lord?* Mack prayed.

God had given Moses a few good tricks up his sleeve, divine wonders to back up his authority when folks wouldn't listen. All Mack had was a good brain, a fine church, a well-stocked provision post that would soon be the region's best general store and the sheer determination to keep another man from climbing to his death. A loud crash assailed Mack's ears, and he wondered how much longer he could hold out without help soon.

Ignoring the shouts, Mack turned his steps toward home. *Please, Lord,* he prayed, ashamed to be driven to such a plea, *let him be asleep. I'm worn out and nothing good'll happen if I snap at the little feller.* For all the nights Mack had walked the village praying protection over its residents, for all the dangers he'd faced in countless adventures, it struck him odd that he'd been reduced to praying for protection against the ravages of a two-year-old.

Mack looked awful when he walked out of his bedroom door the next morning. He rubbed his neck and winced, hair sticking up in all directions and a thick stubble covering his chin. He resembled not so much as man as a foul-mooded bear.

"You made coffee." He said it with a foggy awe that made Lana hide a smile behind the plate she was holding.

"Much needed, don't you think?"

Mack nodded, settling himself at the table and giving the very perky Georgie an analytical eye. Lana set the steaming mug down in front of him and he very nearly clutched it. "If I say I've just discovered the best part about being married, will you hit me with that?"

She eyed the dented tin plate she was holding,

thankful she'd talked Mack into letting her order a new set of china in Skaguay. "Not likely."

He made a dark sound, and she turned to find his gaze aimed out the window to where sheets were hanging. "Why are they out to…?" Lana gulped as Mack turned to level a foul-mooded bear's glare at Georgie. "You didn't."

"It's hardly his fault," Lana angled her body in between them, quieting Georgie's frightened whimper with a bit of the bacon she'd been frying. "He's just barely been trained, and under the circumstances…more coffee?"

Mack laid his forehead into one hand while he held out the already half-drained cup in the other.

They were going to have to soldier through this morning no matter what, so Lana had decided hours ago to put the best face possible on the situation. "There's bacon, eggs, toast and some applesauce Mavis Goodge brought over." She set the full plate in front of him.

"You cook." He seemed troubled by the observation.

"I find eating a rather necessary practice."

Mack took several mouthfuls of egg. "You cook well."

She found the surprise in his voice annoying. Had Jed complained to him about her cooking? "You could be less astonished, you know. And even say thank you if you wanted to really startle me."

This seemed to make him think. "Have you eaten yet?"

"Not really." She'd grown accustomed to snatching her meals in bits and pieces in between feeding and occupying Georgie. The long, luxurious meals they'd had in Skaguay had felt like her first in years.

Mack motioned to the place opposite him at the table. "Sit down. Please." It wasn't a command, it was an invitation. A grumpy, bleary eyed, but genuine attempt at civility. Lana hid her distinct pleasure as she filled a plate and sat down.

And there they were. The three of them, at table, a family. It was familiar and foreign at the same time, given the man at the head of the table. Mack cleared his throat and held out his hands—one to Georgie and one to Lana. She hesitated to give him her hand, ashamed how long it took her to realize what he was about. He was saying grace.

"We give You thanks, Holy Father, for the food You've given us this day. For the blessings we enjoy and the protection we need. May it strengthen us to honor You and Your will today. Amen."

"Amen," Lana said quietly.

"Ugle Ack," Georgie added, batting Mack's hand with the teaspoon he was holding.

Lana waited as long as she could before asking, "Why are you so surprised I can cook? What did Jed say?"

Mack had made short work of the breakfast and

was scraping up the last bits of egg with a corner of his toast. "He said nothing on the matter. It's just that I know you've had house staff most of your life. No reason to learn such things."

"So I'm useless because I grew up with advantages, is that what you're saying?"

"That's not what I'm saying at all. You've just not had much time to learn to fend for yourself. There's cooking to live and then there's good cooking."

Lana sat back and crossed her arms. "And you were thinking you'd just married the kind of woman who can cook enough to keep you alive?"

"I obviously don't know you well enough." He used the diplomatic tone of a man who'd broken up too many arguments.

Lana got up from the table, clearing both their plates. "There's a lot you don't know, Mack Tanner." She reached for the pile of McGuffey Readers she'd poured through in the hours before he woke this morning. She'd started the "Second Year" reader on the boat as they came back from Skaguay, and her opinion had begun to form then. As she sifted through the rest of them this morning—including the pictorial one she started with Georgie last night—the idea had planted itself in her head like a flag thrust in a mountaintop.

As she read through the volumes, Lana discovered she had very definite ideas about education. Ideas about how education was to be accomplished, and by whom, using what techniques. Really, what sort of person launches a child's education with "A is for ax?" Everyone in Treasure Creek was fine with building a school, but it seemed to her no one gave much thought to what would go on inside it, once built. Somewhere in the second half of the "Fifth Year" reader, Lana had the shocking thought that people might assume the Tucker Sisters would simply hammer their last nail and move inside to take up the chalk. Surely not. Nor should they.

"I've read through these," she began.

"Early riser," Mack said, finishing his third cup of coffee.

Lana nodded toward Georgie. "Not by choice." She lay the pile of readers on the table and sat down opposite Mack again. "Who will teach these?"

Mack ran a hand across his chin. "School's not even finished yet. When it is, we'll send word and the government will send out a teacher."

So he didn't have someone in mind for the position. She'd mentally catalogued Treasure Creek's population earlier this morning, and came up with no clear candidate, either.

"I expect one of the Tuckers might even take it on."

Lana swallowed a disparaging laugh. "The Tuckers? Teach school? I doubt that, and I doubt most folks would take to the kind of teaching they'd do anyway. If you want families, we'll need a good school. And these books are a start, I suppose, but…" An hour ago she'd been so sure of what she wanted. Faced with proposing it to Mack, she felt her conviction waver. Alaskan women face life head-on, she reminded herself. Head-on it would be. "I've been thinking about it since I read through these, and, well, I'd like to be our schoolteacher. Very much." Seeing as the world didn't cave in on itself with the voicing of the thought, Lana went on. "And I don't think we should wait until the building's done. There are plenty of places to gather the children we've got. Even the church would work. Or outside on nice days. It's not as if there are crops to get in, and most of these children are sorely lacking in education as it is. We'd only need to meet for an hour or two each day over the summer and it would do them so much good."

Mack said nothing for a long moment, his face an exasperating neutral that offered no clue as to what he thought of the idea.

Georgie chose that moment to knock his bowl onto the floor, sending bits of apple and a chunk of cheese scattering across the cabin floor. On the one hand she was grateful for something to divert her attention from Mack's uncomfortable silence. On the other hand, she didn't care for Georgie's commentary on the proposal.

"You want to teach," he replied when she finished picking up Georgie's spill. His tone was perfectly even. No wonder Jed often said it was a pity Mack shunned cards—the man's face was unreadable.

She returned to her seat at the table. "Yes." Lana

gave her voice what she hoped was command. "I do." Mack pinched the bridge of his nose. Not an encouraging response. Lana counted to ten, willing her hands not to fidget. "Well?"

"I can't say I'm overly fond of the idea."

"Why not?"

Georgie threw his spoon to the ground, babbling. Mack raised an eyebrow at her as if to say he thought she had her hands full already.

She did, but in some twisted way that was part of the attraction of teaching for her. Tending to Georgie was like tidying up after a tornado all day long, only to do it again tomorrow. She desperately needed to feel a sense of accomplishment, of achieving something beyond mere survival. The truth of it was she was as surprised as Mack at the idea, but it had grabbed hold of her somewhere between the fourth and fifth reader and refused to let go. She knew she needed this. She also knew she'd find a way—no matter how hard or complicated—to make it work.

"A man provides for his family. It takes a lot to keep a household running up here. You'll be too busy. I want Georgie to come first."

She'd been worried he would think she couldn't do it. The idea that he thought she *shouldn't* do it pulled something dark and angry out from the hard knot under her stomach. It leapt from her mouth before she could think better of it. "Georgie? Or you?"

"Lana…"

"I'm to fill my days being Mrs. Mack Turner, is that it?"

"You're to be a mother to your son." His voice rose to match hers. "Let someone else, without that kind of responsibility, see to the teaching. The government will send one if we ask. I see no reason for you to take this on. I just don't think it's wise."

"Oh, and you're Mack Tanner—you always know what's best."

Mack pushed away from the table. "We've been married—what?—not even three days? Do you even know what's ahead of you? Of us?"

"I know the timing's not perfect."

"Perfect? It's lunacy. The school's not even built. It's June. Georgie's a handful on a good day. I don't see how this makes any sense." He looked at her, a sharp shadow of hurt behind his eyes. "Isn't this enough?"

Hadn't she asked that very question of herself? A dozen times over? Why, after resisting for months and finally relenting to the one thing she'd thought she'd never do, did she need something else? And she did. She needed this. In a fierce, defiant way she could never begin to describe. It was, she supposed, a way of hanging on to Lana Bristow before she became completely swallowed up by Mrs. Mack Turner. "Not yet" was the only reply she could manage, weak as it was.

Chapter Six

Mack pushed the floorboard into place with his boot. "So I told her I'd think on it."

Ed Parker, down off the trail, in between prospecting trips, hauled more board over from the stack at the far end of the new general store's main room. "You did, did you? Why'd you say that?"

Mack held the board in place with one foot while he nailed the edge down. "Because she loved the idea. She was all fired up and ready to fight for it. I hadn't even seen the sun go down twice on our house and already things are—" he searched for a word "—complicated."

"Nothing complicated about it. Say 'no' and that'll be end of it."

Because that wouldn't be the end of it. He'd seen it in her eyes. This notion had a hold of her and she wasn't about to let it go. Logic didn't come into it. The most he could hope for was to hold off until her head cleared. "You married, Ed?"

Ed dropped the stack of boards with a smirk. "Nope."

"Well, when you've got to spend every morning sitting across from a woman you've said no to, then you come and give me advice, okay?" Mack drove the final nail home.

Ed pulled another board off the stack and slid it up against the one Mack had just secured. "You ain't been married but a few days. What do you know about all that stuff anyways?"

Mack pound in the next nail. "That's the secret to my success. I learn fast."

"I suppose I shouldn't be surprised, seeing as you've got a teacher for a wife and all. Me, I think you have a lot to learn."

"Mack!" Any further commentary was cut short by the appearance of Caleb Johnson. "Got another one for you."

Mack set down his hammer and straightened up with a groan. "Sixth this month. I thought we'd see more of these in winter than now." He walked out of the general store's framed-out shell to see a scrawny young man in tattered shoes and nowhere near enough clothing for the trail's demanding weather. "What's your name, son?"

"David Mindown, sir. Out of Seattle. Came up two weeks ago."

It was the Seattle ones that always showed up like this. Young men who'd hopped the next boat, so sure of their fortune, only to discover how cruel the

Chilkoot Trail could be. Mack was surprised he'd lasted this long. "How old are you, Mindown?"

"Twenty-one."

Mack doubted he'd seen twenty, from the looks of him. "Got family back in Seattle, do you?"

The boy just nodded. The ones that came back down off the trail—especially the ones Caleb brought to him—would almost choke up at the mention of home and family. Most of them were so broken down and hungry they'd been known to call any woman who offered them a good meal and a bit of care "Mother."

"Got anything left at all?"

Caleb and the boy shook their heads simultaneously. This boy should have never been allowed up the trail. Harder men than he had barely made it halfway. Mack put a hand on the boy's shoulder, finding it sharp and bony under the thin shirt he wore. "Time to go home, son. Some adventures are better left to other days. You come on by the house tomorrow morning and I'll get you squared away. There's a ship leaving on Tuesday, I'll book you passage. You got a place to sleep and eat until then?"

"Mavis said the shack is open," Caleb answered. Mavis Goodge, the boardinghouse owner in town, had a little bunkhouse out on the back of her property that she'd fixed up for just such circumstances. Treasure Creek had crafted an odd little rescue system. Caleb usually found the wayward miners in need of rescue. Teena Crow often tended to whatever wounds she could with the Tlingit healing ways that were her gift, as the town still had no doctor to speak of. Mavis gave them shelter. Lucy Tucker took it upon herself to feed whomever was housed out in the little shack, so that it wasn't a burden on Mavis. And Mack funded their passage home. Every home and business in Treasure Creek was either sending prospectors up the Chilkoot or catching them when they fell back down, so needs somehow always got met.

Still, no one really saw to the spiritual needs of all those broken men—except the missionary on the trail, Thomas Stone. And still, he was only one man. Treasure Creek needed a real church, which meant the town needed a real pastor with teaching and preaching gifts, not just a fill-in general store owner with good intentions. Mack seemed to see it more clearly with every lost soul who limped down off the mountain.

"Mavis'll set you up for tonight. I'll see you tomorrow then, David Mindown. And don't you bother with anyone who says they'll wire your mama from Skaguay. There's no telegraph from there, only wires that don't lead to anything except your money going into someone else's pocket." The sham was a common one—and one of the hundreds of predatory schemes that led to Mack's vision of a honest town in Treasure Creek.

Ed came up behind him on the General Store's future front steps. "You're too good to kids like that. A fella's got to learn to pull himself up by his own bootstraps. You can't go around scooping 'em up and sending them back home just 'cause they've hit hard times."

Mack looked at the skinny fellow sulking his way down the street beside Caleb. "Hard times is one thing. Freezing to death on the trail is another. You and I both know what they do to pups like that in Skaguay."

"Yep," replied Ed as they both turned back to their work, "but I wish I didn't."

Lana spent the morning organizing the house and cooking Mack a nice picnic lunch. He was working hard keeping his provisions outpost running while building the new general store, and he'd lost time while he took her to Skaguay. Lana thought she owed him the courtesy of a decent meal. Besides, things had been rather cool when he left this morning, and she hoped the gesture might smooth things over.

She'd been so taken with the concept of teaching, it hadn't even occurred to her how broadsided Mack would be by the idea. Even she found it rather sudden. Snapping at him for his honest reaction wasn't the smartest response. Jed hadn't been a champion of honesty in marriage, and she was just coming to understand that honesty sometimes meant you didn't like what you heard.

She made the mistake of stopping by one of

the dockside fruit stalls on her way to the General Store. Treasure Creek's waterfront could be beautiful or chaotic, depending on which ship was docked. "Serves me right," Lana chided herself as she hoisted Georgie up on one hip, for fear of losing him in today's teeming, boisterous crowd. Caleb would have his hands full today; men, animals and crates of every description were piled in disorganized clumps all over the beach and adjoining road. Lana heard four different languages and winced at several bouts of indecent banter as she picked her way through the throng. She had just decided fresh fruit wasn't worth the trouble when a young man sidled up next to her.

"Lemme me carry that for you, ma'am. Looks like quite a load to get through this mob." The double load of toddler and picnic basket had made maneuvering treacherous, if not close to impossible. She vaguely recognized him; he was in his early twenties, clean-cut by Skaguay standards and boasting a charming smile. He tipped his hat at both her and Georgie. "You's Mack's new wife, ain't you?"

"Thank you. I am."

"And you used to be Jed's gal, right?" He took the basket from her arm with one hand, putting the other over his heart. "Shame about Jed. I'm sorry for your loss, but I expect you'll be right happy as Mrs. Tanner. Fine man, Mack Tanner."

"He is indeed." She nodded toward the basket. "That's his lunch you're hauling. And Georgie's."

"And a cute little bug he is, too. You make a pretty family. I expect he treats you right, buys you all kinds of pretty things. A man of such position ought to display his success, I always say."

Something in his turn of phrase, or maybe just slippery edge of his words, made her sorry she'd let him take the basket. "Mack treats me well."

"He should. He can. Generous man, Mack Tanner. 'Course, that's easy to do when you've got a heap of gold to back up your fine sentiments. What I wouldn't give to be his banker, hmm?"

Lana didn't care for the direction of this conversation. "My husband makes no secret of his distrust in banks, Mr...."

"No sir," he replied, ignoring her cue for his name, "I believe I've heard as much." He leaned too close to her, arching one eyebrow in a way that sent a shiver down Lana's back. "Makes a man wonder, though. Where *does* a smart man like your husband keep that heap of gold?" She felt his hand take hold of her elbow. "Jed left you a heap of gold all your own, come to think of it. My, what a fortune the two of you must make. Tell me, does Mack share his hiding places with his pretty little wife? His pretty little rich widow, who wanders the streets alone?"

Lana yanked her hand free and turned on the weasely little man. She snatched the basket from him with all the force she could muster, even though it nearly sent Georgie rocking. "What he shares is none of your business! And the wife of Mack Tanner had best be able to walk anywhere she pleases without foolish threats from the likes of you. I expect if you show your face in Treasure Creek again…" Before she could finish her angry thought, the man had tipped his hat in a sinister fashion and melted back into the bustling crowd around her.

She stood for a shocked, angry moment, gasping and clutching Georgie tight to her side. In all her time up north, even in Jed's days of showing off their wealth, she'd never been threatened like that. Curiosity over the whereabouts of Mack's wealth always fueled gossip in Treasure Creek—even Jed had never known where Mack kept his funds. And Jed hadn't ever hid his wealth, which drew all kinds of hangers-on, but those parasites had showed the good graces to stay away from her. Mostly. It had never fueled something like this. In the middle of town. To her own person.

Marriage was supposed to have kept her from being this kind of target. Instead of afraid, the whole affair made her angry. Marrying Mack was supposed to offer protection, but did it paint a bull's-eye on her back instead? Or—worse yet—Georgie's?

Fuming, Lana pushed her way through the noisy waterfront crowd to the General Store building site. She stomped up the steps to thrust herself and Georgie through the half-framed doorway, casting the basket to the floor with a huff.

"Still sore at me?" Mack's tone was teasing until he saw her face.

"There was a man down on the waterfront. He offered to help me with the basket, and I recognized him. Sort of." She fought the urge to brush off her elbow where he'd grabbed her. "He was nice at first, but then he had the nerve to threaten me."

Mack crossed the large room to her in a handful of steps. "Who threatened you? Why?" His raised voice sent Georgie's lip quivering.

"He assumed you'd told me where you keep your gold. And Jed's. And he made it quite clear that 'a lady of my substantial resources' shouldn't walk the streets by myself."

Mack's face darkened instantly. "Who said this?"

"He looked familiar, but I don't know his name. I've seen him before, I know that much."

"He threatened you because you're married to me?" Mack nearly roared, sending Georgie into tears.

Ed Parker came up behind Mack, "You're frightening the boy, Mack. Hold your horses."

Mack tried to compose himself by turning away and pacing the room. "Of all the underhanded, low-life…" He looked up at Lana. "You said you knew him?"

"I recognized him. I suspect he was an…associate…of Jed's. He didn't offer his name when I asked."

"He knows what's coming to him if I did know his name. You'd know him if you saw him again?"

"I doubt I'll get his sneer out of my head for quite a while."

"Don't you leave," Mack commanded, pointing at both Lana and Ed as he made for the door.

"He slipped back into the crowd, Mack," Lana called. "A block or two back. You won't find him now."

"Watch me," Mack growled, sending Georgie into full-scale howling.

"Must you—"

"Mack!" Ed cut in as he beat Mack to the door frame. "Don't go off all fired up. You won't solve anything like this. He's just some fool out to rattle your cage."

"Consider me rattled." Mack looked back at Lana. "Are you hurt? Georgie? Did he touch you?"

Lana smoothed Georgie's hair, bouncing him up and down gently until his cries muffled down to short bursts of whimpering. "No, he caught hold of my arm for a second, that's all."

"He touched you? I'll wring his neck, I will."

"I'm not hurt, Mack. I refused to be bullied by some low-life miner off the docks."

"That low-life miner could have done any number of things to you. Or Georgie. Thank God above neither of you were hurt."

"He never touched Georgie." She looked straight at Mack. "It's getting worse instead of better, Mack. The boats just keep dumping people out, no matter who they are and what they want."

"Oh, we know what they want, all right. No questions there." Mack drew a deep breath and shrugged his shoulders, grappling to get his temper under control. "I'll find him."

"You will," Ed said. "But not today." Ed turned to Lana. "I'm right glad you're okay after a scare like that. Do you think you could describe him? Anything that might pick him out of a crowd?"

Lana felt her anger return as she brought the slippery character to mind. "He had an accent. Georgia. Or Texas, maybe." She gave all the physical description she could, trying to keep her voice even and calm, to help Georgie settle himself. She opened the picnic basket and pulled out a bit of bread to distract the boy. "His hat had a colored feather in it. Like a peacock's."

"The fool. Thinking he can do that to you." Mack continued pacing, his voice low but still menacing. "You go nowhere alone. You understand that? Nowhere."

That wasn't the answer. "Mack, I'm not some orchid who has to be guarded," Lana countered. "He scared me, but I've lived here as long as you, and nothing's ever happened before."

"You haven't been Mrs. Tanner before," he shot back.

She had been Mrs. Jedadiah Bristow. That had been education enough. "And I've no mind to be imprisoned for that!"

"I'll not have you putting yourself in danger."

His overprotective response made her almost sorry she'd told him of the incident. "One fool thinking he can scare me is not danger."

"You don't know that, Lana."

"It's only worse when the waterfront is mobbed like that."

"So you stay off the waterfront. Until further notice." His annoying, paternal tone had her thinking he'd wag a finger at her in another second.

"I already planned to do just that. When the big ships are in."

"At *all* times."

"Mack—"

"A man just threatened you, Lana, and I will not have you taking a chance like that again." Georgie's whimper returned and Mack visibly reined in his temper. "Not even to bring me lunch." After a moment, he added, "Thank you for bringing me lunch, all the same. It smells wonderful."

He was making an effort, reluctant as it was. Perhaps she ought to as well. "There's enough for you, Mr. Parker." In her exuberance—and the joy of having more than enough supplies to cook anything she wanted after so many weeks of scraping by— she'd probably made enough for four.

"I may not be a scholar, but I know enough to leave two newlyweds alone. Even arguin' ones. How about I take Georgie over to the carpenters and see if I can find some scraps we can make into blocks?" He looked at Georgie. "You got any blocks yet, fella? Every boy needs blocks." Despite Lana's certainty that Georgie wouldn't go two feet from her after all the fuss, Georgie toddled over to the big man's outstretched hand.

"Mind him, Ed," Mack called after the unlikely pair. "He misses his own nephews, I think," Mack remarked to Lana. "He's a big old teddy bear on the inside."

She managed a laugh. "You'd never know it to look at him."

"He's had a rough life. Seen a lot—both good and bad. He's been a good friend, though, since…" He gave a forced sigh and settled himself on the store floor, sunlight streaming in around them through the still open framework on one side of the building. Some days she could be so swallowed up by the loss of her husband of three years that she would clean forget Mack had lost his best friend of nearly thirty years. How two such different men could grow up together and still stay friends always amazed her.

She looked up at the grief shadowing Mack's eyes and sighed. They still didn't quite know how to be alone in a room together. Lana occupied herself by unfolding a napkin. "We've all had a rough night. Tempers are short."

He made a low grunt in reply and rubbed his neck. "Smells mighty good," he admitted, as the scent of the chicken wafted through the room.

She filled a tin plate and handed it to him. "I'm a very capable person, you know."

He looked up, a *what's that supposed to mean?* expression in his eyes.

"I'm smart enough to know what's possible and what isn't." She filled a plate for herself. "For example, I am smart enough to know that I can't make it up here alone, but I am also smart enough to know that I can teach those books."

His eyes flicked up from the food, but he said nothing.

Lana settled her plate on her lap and deliberately softened her tone. She waited for the tension to ebb from the room, watching instead how the crisp ribbons of sunlight illuminated the bits of sawdust dancing on the waterfront breeze. Keeping her tone as soft as she knew how, Lana caught his eyes. "Tell me why you don't like the idea of my teaching."

He gave the question considerable thought before replying. "I think," he chose his words carefully, "that your plate is full enough already. If you'll pardon the lunch reference," he added with the barest hint of a smile. "And then there's Georgie. I don't see how you could do it."

"Well, I don't know much of that myself yet." He obviously hadn't expected such an answer, for he stared hard at her, as if she were some difficult puzzle he couldn't solve. It was true. She felt like a puzzle to herself today.

"You don't need the job. You're provided for now."

"I don't need the money, true. But I think I need

the challenge. There's a right way to do this." The ambitious urge those books pulled out of her caught her by surprise, much as that hideous miner had this morning. "I want Treasure Creek to have a good school for Georgie. I want everyone here to have a good school."

"And you've a definite opinion on how that ought to happen." He declared it like an unfortunate fact of nature, like floods or avalanches.

"I do. And you're right, I know the why but not the how. At least not yet. So…" She put a luxurious slather of butter on her biscuit, "I'd like to try and work it out. I don't think asking you to keep an open mind about this is too much." She looked up and caught his eye again, pleased to see the dark storm of anger had retreated considerably, replaced with a rather amusing curiosity. If there was anything Lana Bristow Tanner knew how to do best, it was to coax a deal into existence. "In return, I'll keep an open mind about your ideas of what's needed for my safety."

He managed an actual smile. "Those marriage vows had 'honor' in them, and some other words, but I don't recall much about 'keep an open mind.'"

He'd left out the bit about "obey," and they both knew it. Lana sat up straight. "An open mind is the highest honor a man can give his wife."

Her statement amounted to a well-played verbal parry, and Mack raised a dubious eyebrow before dissolving into a smirk. They both laughed. It was the first time they'd laughed together, and the first time Lana could remember laughing in ages. There was a precious warmth to it. It was—dare she think it?—fun to coax a deal out of him. He matched her efforts by displaying his "consideration" with an oversize thinking expression while devouring a piece of chicken. His dark blue eyes had hints of gold and green in them when the light hit them right. She'd thought of them as a flat, stormy blue, but there was a shimmer in the storm she hadn't noticed before. Yes, he did have a playful side. One she'd all but forgotten in the onslaught of drama and conflict that had been both their lives. Georgie would be good for him. Shake some of that stiffness out of him in the way that only small children can.

"I will honor you by keeping an open mind," he said too formally, "but I reserve the right to put my foot down. 'Obey' was in there somewhere."

It wasn't much, but it was all she needed. "Fair enough."

"You'll not set foot on the waterfront again today." There was no play in that; it was a clear command.

"And you'll walk me home just to make certain of that." It wasn't a request, it was an admission. An acceptance of the limits of his tolerance. The seal of the deal, as it were.

Chapter Seven

The weasel. Mack was all too happy to toss that peacock-feathered lowlife onto the next boat out of Treasure Creek. He should have tossed his banker friend right behind him. It was a wonder anyone kept any of their gold dust, with what passed for bankers up here. The only thing "safe" at any of these banks was the giant steel box they locked up at night. After walking Lana and Georgie home following their lunch, it hadn't taken much poking around the waterfront with Caleb to find "Nick Peacock" and ensure he had a one-way passage out of town. As he'd been foolish enough to threaten Lana, Mack doubted he was smart enough to be working on his own. He wasn't. He'd been working with Lester Jameson, the slipperiest banker Treasure Creek had. That partnership officially took things from bad to worse, and Lana was going to need more protection whether she liked it or not.

He reached his door and stopped short at what now hung above the latch. Someone had put a nail in his door and hung a little handmade sign on it. Made from a scrap of hide and hung from an alarmingly bright purple ribbon, it read "Quiet! Sleeping Child!" with a frilly little flower drawn below the words. It had the look, he realized with a thud in his stomach, of something intended for repeated use. She'd hung the curtains they'd bought in Skaguay, too. He hadn't counted on the new feminine touches to his house bothering him so. Reminding himself that "feminine" also brought the very good chicken he'd had for lunch, Mack lifted the door latch as quietly as possible.

The house smelled like woman. There wasn't another way to describe it. Floral, soft scents filled the rooms. Little bottles of things were everywhere, and it seemed like every flat surface was covered with something ruffled. Irritation vied with amusement as he took in both his altered house and her pleased expression. Lana had been busy.

She pointed to the shut door of the room she shared with Georgie, a grin on her face as she made the universal sleeping symbol of folded hands tucked under her cheek. Mack took extreme care to set down the box he was holding as quietly as he could. "We need to talk," he whispered.

Lana took a glance at the closed bedroom door. "Outside," she whispered back, pointing to the front door.

This wasn't a conversation Mack wanted to have on his front step, but this wasn't a conversation that could wait, either. And it would be easier to talk frankly about the dangers without Georgie's tender ears around.

Once out the door, he led Lana around to the side of the house. As they walked past Georgie's blue-curtained windows, Mack pulled the window open and propped it with an inch-high stick. "Now we'll hear him if he wakes," he explained to Lana as he turned the corner to the small yard that backed the house. Lana had been busy here, too. Two patches of land on either side of the yard been staked out and turned over. Mrs. Tanner expected to garden, it seemed. It was a good idea; the nearly full days of sunlight—up to twenty hours at the peak—made growing things easy and fast. Still, he couldn't tell if her quick efforts to make herself at home pleased him or unsettled him. Probably both.

"I found your nasty little friend." It was best to get straight to the point. Georgie could wake up at any moment. "Nicky Peacock will think twice before he talks to you again."

Lana looked shocked. "What did you do to him?"

Mack had, in fact, done too much to him. If he'd heeded Caleb's warnings, he might have stopped after the first punch. As it was, Mack let his temper get the best of him, and he'd given Nicky Peacock a fair beating before Caleb pulled him off and told him to go home. Many in Treasure Creek saw him as the law, and the moment he'd walked away from the young man God had convicted him of how wrong he'd been to make his point with his fists. Treasure Creek was no place for thugs, but Treasure Creek didn't need him to become one to protect it, either. "More than I ought to," was all he admitted to Lana. "Sang like a bird after the third punch, though, so something good came from it, I suppose."

Lana pushed away the wisps of hair the breeze had flung in her face. "What do you mean?"

"Lester Jameson put him up to it. I thought as much. Peacock's not sharp enough to think of something like that on his own."

"Jameson? The banker Jed used to use?"

Mack leaned up against the sun-warmed side of the house. "The same. Probably thought I'd view his bank as a more viable option if I felt lowlifes would use you to get to my gold."

Lana's eyebrows scrunched up as she followed Jameson's line of thinking. "So he thinks you'll put your gold in his bank if you think miners would threaten me? He was Jed's banker—he must know Jed left me with almost nothing. Why does everyone suddenly think I know where you've hidden your gold? Even if I did, who would trust someone who would resort to such things?"

Mack folded his hands across his chest. "You'd be surprised. Everybody's suspicious of everyone else in the camps. With reason. Get a man away from home long enough, give him enough gold to do foolish things and crave more, and sense goes out the window." He leaned back against the house. "If men staked their claim, made their fortunes and went home, it'd be one thing. But it's like a disease. Suddenly nothing's enough, and no scheme's too slippery if it leads to more gold." He watched her expression, knowing too well they both counted Jed among those men who'd left their common sense somewhere out there on the trail. "Nicky's just a dumb kid with a smooth tongue. I don't think he'd actually have hurt you. Jameson, on the other hand, is a dangerous snake. He'll keep trying."

Lana hugged her chest. "But you'd never trust him now. He knows that."

"No, he doesn't. And I won't tell him."

She turned to look at him. "You didn't go beat *him* up the minute you heard?"

Mack walked over to the spade that lay against the house and began banging it softly against his boots to knock off the thick layer of mud. "Some men are safer fooled. I put Nicky on the ferry to Skaguay with my own two fists, and told Caleb to make sure he never finds passage again. I told Nicky that Jameson would have him shot if he admitted to squealing to me, which might even be true. No, it's better if Jameson never knows how much I know. Then he'll keep thinking his foolish tricks will work, and never try anything more sinister." After a moment he added. "I hope."

He'd just finished banging the mud off the other boot when Lana straightened up, turned to him and asked, "Well, where *is* your gold?"

"What?" He'd nearly bellowed it out in his shock that she'd even ask—but she glared at him and pointed to Georgie's window. "Do you really think I'd tell you?" he said in a lower voice. "After what happened today?" She had gumption, that woman. He had to give her that much.

"I *am* your wife."

She had an infuriating way of saying things that made no sense, but saying them in a way that made him feel foolish for not understanding. As if their married state made it obvious why she should have such dangerous information. Only one person on earth knew where Mack's gold was, and that was Mack himself. And it was going to stay that way, especially now. "My gold is safe, and that's all you need to know."

Her scowl would be amusing on such delicate features if it didn't look so heart-felt. "We're supposed to be partners in life. This isn't going to work if you don't trust me. And it's rather obvious that you don't trust me."

"What I don't trust," he said as he thrust the shovel into the ground beside him, "is the long line of rascals who'd do anything to make you betray that trust. It's *better* if you don't know. I'd think today would have made that clear." When that failed to unfurrow her brow, he added, "I have a plan to handle this."

She huffed at that. "And I will not be told what that plan is?"

"It's best that way, yes."

"For whom?"

Mack looked up to heaven while leaning back against the wall again, questioning God for having ever called him to complicate his life with this woman. "Lana, have you ever heard the old saying, 'he who has the gold makes the rules'?"

Her hands planted themselves on her hips with another huff. "I prefer the other golden rule, thank you. The one about treating others the way you'd like to be treated. The one from the Bible. If you'll excuse me, I believe I hear Georgie waking up."

He hadn't heard a peep from the room around the corner, but he sure wasn't going to let that get in the way of her quick strides away from him. He'd known she was a handful when he proposed marriage— even the sixth time—but he'd underestimated just how ornery the woman could be. Mack pulled the shovel from its place in the dirt, only to thrust it back in again, frustrated. He wasn't about to let her turn this into some kind of test, some linchpin on which to hang the success of their marriage. Men didn't play by the rules here. Treasure Creek was becoming a place where decency and fair play were expected, but that hardly meant everyone lived up to expectations. They wouldn't just stop looking for his gold any more than Georgie would stop looking for cookies…until Ed gave him blocks.

Distraction.

Could it really be that simple? Could he throw the worst of the fortune hunters off his trail by providing another, easier target? Mack squatted down, running his hands over the upturned soil at his feet while he pondered the idea. By the time someone found a decoy treasure he could create and place in easy reach, attention over Lana's bridal status would have died down. That might buy him time to squelch any false rumors about Jed's bequest to Lana. Could he find a way to disclose that Jed had died nearly penniless and still keep Lana's reputation intact? It was possible, given time. More time would also let him think about how to handle the rest of his gold in a way that dealt with the complications of his new family. And the demands of his new wife. It was all a matter of crafting the right plan.

By the time she called him in for supper, Mack had not only fenced in his wife's new garden, he'd worked out all the details of his new plan.

Lana looked up from her list after dinner to steal a glimpse of Mack as he sat on the hearth rug. He was helping Georgie play with the blocks Ed had gotten for him. She didn't know whether to be pleased or annoyed that he'd taken them away from Georgie to sand them after dinner. Georgie had understandably screamed at this, but Mack firmly announced that

Ed missed too many of the sharper edges. Disaster loomed until Georgie found the sanding sound hysterical, giggling as if the *scratch-scratch* ticked his ears. Now she was watching Mack make a big show of sanding each one, handing it to Georgie when it passed final inspection. "All smooth," he said, running Georgie's finger down the edge of the final block, a big triangle.

"Oov," Georgie repeated, grabbing Mack's finger to do the same, then holding the block up to her with a triumphant grin. "Oov, Mama!"

"That's right. Go show Mama your new blocks," Mack's voice pitched to a groan as he hauled his large frame off the floor. "What's that?" Mack pointed to the list Lana had been creating.

"It's a list of students. I figure we have eleven in town now, and I wouldn't be surprised if that doubles by the time the fall comes. Folks are clamoring for a decent school up here. It will make Treasure Creek a very desirable place to live. If you get school up and running even a few days a week over the summer, more families will settle in before winter."

"I hadn't thought about it like that. A schoolhouse under construction is good, but actual lessons could be even better I suppose." Mack sat down and ran his finger over the list.

"The first number is their age," Lana explained. "The second is my guess at which reader they'll use."

He sat back in the chair. "You'll need more of the first- and second-year books."

She smiled, feeling the victory sparkle down her spine. "*I* will?"

"You will."

"You're agreeing to let me teach?"

"I prefer to say I've honored my promise to keep an open mind."

Lana nearly gasped. Jed had broken so many promises to her that she'd forgotten how good it would feel to have Mack keep one of his. Lana flipped to another page in what she'd begun to call her "Lesson Planner."

"One hour, two days a week," she said as she showed him the little calendar she'd drawn. "That's all we need to start." She actually welcomed the idea of partnering with him, surprising as it was. "You can announce it at church on Sunday and— thank you, Georgie—our first class can be Tuesday." Georgie began handing blocks to her and to Mack in turns, sharing his new toys between them. Like they were a real family.

Mack eyed her. "You've got it all—thank you, Georgie—worked out, haven't you?"

"Yes, and I'm *sharing* my plan *with* you. See how this works?"

He made that grunting sound she had come to understand as *I'm not going to answer that.* She was just about to offer her commentary when Georgie beat her to it: he looked at Mack and made a perfectly ridiculous grunt about two octaves higher.

Mack had the good sense to look outnumbered, muttered something about his evening walk and grabbed his hat.

Chapter Eight

Lana should not know anything about the gold or its location. Mack told himself that over and over as he went on his nightly walk around Treasure Creek. They didn't have that kind of a marriage to start with—it wasn't as if he was depriving her of some kind of promised intimacy. This marriage had been about protection from the start. It shouldn't stop being about protection just because she was relentless.

She was too bold. What might have happened if anyone smarter than Nicky Peacock had been pressed into service to threaten her? The trouble with Lana was that she didn't know how much she *didn't* know. She probably thought she'd seen the worst of Jed's behavior back before he died. The truth of the matter was that Mack had gone to great lengths to hide the worst of Jed's behavior. Jameson was far from the darkest of Jed's "associates." Jed not only died penniless, as Lana thought, but he died deep in debt—and to some of the Yukon's most unsavory lenders. Lana had no idea how many of Jed's debts Mack had paid off, and it was best if it stayed that way. She should never know that if Mack hadn't stepped in, there was a good chance she'd be dead.

The purple-blue calm of Alaska's bright evenings—it was near ten and still just barely sunset—worked the knots out of Mack's spirit as he walked. He heard laughter from the Tucker sisters' cabin, and said a prayer of thanks for the sturdy women's work on the schoolhouse. He prayed protection over the new baby down the street. A baby was a rare joy up here, and one to be celebrated. He walked past the lamp in Ed Parker's front window and thanked God for that new friendship. It helped to fill the yawning gap Jed left when he died. As much trouble as Jed had been, Mack was fond of the man's adventurous spirit and endless optimism. He'd promenaded like a dandy with Lana, up and down the first boardwalk they'd built in Treasure Creek, casting grand visions of the many businesses that would spring up along the road. Back then it was a muddy swath of a path, but listening to Jed, one could almost see the town growing out of the mist. Jed had insisted on being the first customer at every new business—even when Mack had to lend him the gold to do it. As much as it used to drive him crazy,

Mack missed Jed's impulsive theatrical nature. Even when he bore the disastrous consequences. When Georgie made faces at him as the boy did just now, he would see Jed in Georgie's eyes. *They'll be safe now, Jed, I promise you that.*

He'd made promises to Lana, too, hadn't he? Mack heard the thought in Lana's voice inside his head, a sensation so startling he actually shuddered. *Honor does not mean share everything,* he argued. A man could "cherish and honor" his wife in ways that weren't likely to get her killed. Women liked gifts and fine words and such things, they didn't need secrets to feel... He stopped himself from finishing that sentence with the word "loved." It didn't apply here. If God was kind, they'd come to a mutual respect, a fortunate affection of sorts, but this wasn't a romance. Still, Lana had always been appeased—dare he even say "distracted"—by pretty things.

It reminded him to check in at the post office for something he was expecting from Skaguay. A blazing fire told him Duncan MacDougal, the Scottish blacksmith who'd somehow also taken up a position as Treasure Creek's postmaster, was still up and working. It had seemed pure foolishness to let a man who worked with fire also keep the mail—the threat of Treasure Creek's full correspondence going up in smoke gave Mack nightmares for two weeks—but Duncan was an avid stamp collector, and as such pressed Mack endlessly for the unlikely dual position.

That was the trouble with a place like Treasure Creek. Only the most headstrong, relentless types ever made it this far and fewer still were stubborn enough to stay. The town could be the bravest on earth, but it could also be the most bullheaded place under Heaven.

"Duncan?" Mack poked his head into the steaming heat of the blacksmith shop.

"Mack! I was going to come see ye in the mornin'." The man pulled a bandana from his overalls and wiped his forehead. "Your package arrived from Skaguay. Looks fancy. Get something nice for the new missus on your honeymoon, hmm?"

Mack said nothing about the honeymoon comment, but only nodded.

Duncan thrust a twisted arc of orange metal into a hissing bucket of water and shucked the heavy glove off his hand. "Got it on the other side for ye." They walked together to the other side of Duncan's cabin, for at Mack's insistence, Duncan's wide cabin separated the post office and the blacksmith shop. "Heard you're sending young Mindown on his way. Can't say I'm surprised. I can almost tell which ones'll make it just by lookin' at them now."

"I can, too—" Mack shrugged "—although occasionally one will surprise me. Not Mindown."

"No, sir, not Mindown. He's not for this kind of

life, that's for sure. Better off outside." "Outside" was a local term for anything nonlocal. Essentially, "outside" was anywhere south and civilized, and Duncan was right, "outsiders" always had a look about them he could spot a mile off.

Duncan handed him the package, a wide grin splitting his red mustache and beard as he said something in Scottish. "Long and happy life to ye, Mack. Congratulations to you and the new Mrs. Tanner."

Step one had been accomplished. Mack walked for another half hour in widening circles around the town, the package heavy in his left coat pocket, before he veered off the streets and ducked into the woods beside the Chilkoot trail to accomplish step two. Twenty minutes later, he walked back down the street toward home with his right coat pocket equally bulging with six gold nuggets from his own private fortune. He'd invent some sort of story of a long-hidden settler's treasure, and greedy imaginations would take it from there.

Distraction was a good strategy indeed.

Lana was still poring over books when he returned to the cabin. Georgie made so much commotion while awake that the place always seemed doubly peaceful once he went to sleep. Finally dark and near midnight, the small hearth fire filled the room with a golden glow. She'd made tea; he could smell its tang even before he saw the china cup on the table beside her. She'd insisted on at least one real teacup to hold her over until the china arrived from Seattle. Mack's big hands would never manage the delicate cups, and, as he preferred coffee anyway, some tin mugs would remain, even when the tin plates gave way to patterned china. He secretly hoped their arrival would be delayed, as too much of his store stock had already been.

"I stopped by to see Duncan on my walk." He pulled the package from his coat pocket when he hung up his hat. "I had something made for you while we were in Skaguay, and it's arrived."

She closed the book and set it on her lap as she glanced up. She looked like such a lady, perched on that chair by the fire, tea and book at her side. She could have been anywhere in any fancy city, her hair piled high and her lacy collar frothy around her neck like that, but she was here in his house. Just now, as it did every once in a while since they'd married, the unlikeliness of it all struck him. He was a married man. Married to this beautiful woman. Despite the tea and the strange scents and the constant cluttered commotion of Georgie, there was something admittedly nice about coming home to…well, to *her*. And the food? Well, he just hadn't counted on how good that would be.

He handed the package to her. "I suppose I should

have had them put it in some kind of pretty box or something, but I didn't think of it 'til just now."

She smiled, and the radiance did something to him he hadn't expected. Lana loved presents more than any adult he'd ever met. "It's just fine the way it is."

Normally, when Mack set a plan in motion, he rarely had a second thought. His endeavors were so carefully thought out that regrets or doubts never entered the picture. And when he'd had this made, it seemed the perfect gesture. Suddenly, as she worked the all-too-plain brown wrapper off the package, Mack felt an unfamiliar pang of anxiety. Had he done the wrong thing?

He watched her every move as she unfolded the soft cloth around the brooch. It was a delicate sunburst pattern, two thin four-pointed stars overlaid on a lacy background. Filigree, the jeweler had called it, with a small colored stone set in the tip of each point. He'd seen it in the window of a shop, and while it was the same size and shape as the brooch she'd always worn, it was different in style. It seemed like a good way to replace her broken pin, the one Jed had given her on their third anniversary back when he was flush with gold. The one Georgie had broken the day she'd said yes to being Mrs. Mack Tanner. This bauble gave her something like the old, but still new. Not much of a man for symbolism, the gesture seemed to say what he wanted to say to her about their life together. Replacing the old broken one as best he could, but knowing it could never be repaired completely.

It had seemed such a wise token then. It seemed pure folly now. He drew in a breath to explain his thinking, then realized to say the thoughts out loud would make them sound even more foolish.

Lana was very, very quiet. He was thankful she didn't look up, for he was afraid to see her eyes. She ran her fingers around the oval shape of it, and he knew she recognized the similar shape of her old brooch. What ever made him think that was a good idea? He'd always been awful at this sort of thing. It seemed impossible to know if she would smile or run from the room in tears.

She did both. When she finally looked up—which seemed like a dozen years—her eyes were brimmed with tears, but she smiled. A broken, unsteady smile, but a smile all the same. "A new one," she said softly. Usually a sharp judge of character, Mack was completely unable to gauge her response.

"Do you like it?" he asked, then wanted to whack his forehead for the clumsy, boyish question. He realized he dreaded her answer either way.

"It looks almost like a golden compass, doesn't it?" Her remark was overbright and forced.

"I thought, since your old one is broken…" Again, why were such foolish thoughts jumping out of his mouth?

"Yes," she said quickly, as if to stop him from finishing the sentence. She swallowed hard, and he felt it lodge in his own chest. Trying to replace Jed's pin had been an arrogant mistake. "Thank you," she said after another telling gulp of air. She gathered up the package and stood up. "Thank you," she said again, and only just barely managed to add "Good night," before she went into the room she shared with Georgie and shut the door. She left her teacup half full on the table.

Mack stood for a long moment, staring at the forgotten cup and feeling like God's greatest fool for trying to patch up something as large as the death of a man, the loss of a husband, with a chunk of gold. *A golden compass. Gold, you idiot, the very thing that led Jed to his death. What were you thinking?*

As he picked up the teacup and rinsed it carefully, Mack heard the dagger-sharp, chest-splitting sound of his wife trying to cry quietly. He could kid himself only for a second that it was to keep Georgie from waking. He knew that truly, it was to keep him from hearing what a great, heartless fool he'd been.

Lana held one of her beloved handkerchiefs tight against her mouth and rocked back and forth on the little chest at the foot of her bed. The kind cruelty of Mack's gift seem to stab straight into the heart of her grief. She'd loved Jed, faults and all. That love

had been all but crushed, but this gift made her realize there was still some part of her who loved that
broken man. Some remnant of her heart that would
always love the father of her child, the adventurer,
the dreamer.

Still, she'd been broken by his love, damaged by
his reckless nature, just as Georgie had damaged
the brooch. Not malicious, but lethal just the same.
To trade one pin for the other seemed somehow to
kill the first dream of that dashing adventurous life
and surrender it to the harsh realities of her life now.
Not that she hadn't realized that once she said yes
to Mack's proposal, but it seemed so much more
real, now that she'd retrieved the bent pin from its
place in the back of her jewelry chest and sat with
the two brooches in front of her.

How was it that Jed's brooch had become such
a talisman to her, so potent a symbol of the life
she was supposed to have had? The fact that Mack
attempted to replace it was a tender cruelty. He
must have known the deep meaning of the gift—
he couldn't have picked such a gift without understanding what he'd done. He was strong and could
face such harsh truths head-on. To Lana, it seemed
to lay her grief and dependency open, exposing her
wounds.

If he'd knowingly lanced the wound wide open,
intending to heal, did he know how very deep a cut
he'd made?

* * *

Light was already coming into the room when Lana closed her bedroom door softly and padded out into the main room. She had a shawl wrapped around her shoulders, wore a simple blouse and skirt and her hair wasn't done up as usual, but rather tied back in a plain loose braid. Yet still, she had a rare grace about her. Mack had been up for hours, already slumped in the chair by the dying fire, trying to make sense of the rattling in his brain. And failing. Failing to make sense of anything.

She looked like she'd slept about as much as he did—which was not at all. If marrying Lana was the right thing to do, why was this so hard? Why did trying to make it better seem to only result in more pain for everyone? He had always been inept at romantic gestures, and maybe that was the problem. This wasn't a romance. It couldn't be, not with all the water under the bridge between them. Still, he'd hoped the pin would symbolize a fresh start of sorts, but it was clear it hadn't done anything of the sort. Maybe a fresh start wasn't possible just now. "Good morning," he said softly, as she padded toward the kitchen, realizing she hadn't even seen him sitting in the shadows.

She stilled and looked up like a startled fawn, her face pale and her lips drawn tight. It only took a second—maybe not even that—but he watched her apply another, more public face and pull her shoulders upright. "I'll get breakfast started. Georgie will be up soon." She looked upward, as if plucking a safe topic of conversation out of the air, and asked, "Do I need to have breakfast ready early tomorrow? I don't know what time you need to be at church. Do you get there long before we do?" Mack was filling the pulpit as best he could, but even his basic skills and strong desire to shepherd this fledgling flock wouldn't suffice much longer. Especially at the rate Treasure Creek was growing. Men's spirits broke as fast as their bones up on the Chilkoot, and the town's spiritual life was too important not to be one man's sole priority.

She rummaged through the kitchen with her back to him. It was clear she didn't want to discuss last night. He thought they should, but as he didn't yet have the slightest notion what to do about any of it, maybe some time to sort things out wasn't a bad plan. "An hour before," he said, rising and pulling his suspenders back into place. One was forever falling down because it was in bad repair.

"If you give those to me, I'll get them fixed for you," she said, gesturing toward the suspenders with the spatula she held. "We should have gotten you a new pair in Skaguay. Seems silly to have done all that shopping for only Georgie and me." The mention of Skaguay and shopping, however, seem to pull the conversation toward the gift, and neither of them wanted that. She sliced off a bit of bacon and with a slight shake of her head, switched topics again. "I've written down what folks need to know about the session of school. I can give it to you after breakfast. That way you'll have plenty of time to think about how you'll announce it."

"I'll announce it," he agreed. He'd come to see that the trial school session was in fact a very good idea. Worth trying, even if it did make him uncomfortable about how Lana's involvement and the logistics would work out. "I'll be out most of the morning." It was odd, having to let someone else know his plans for the day. He still couldn't decide if he liked it—part of him enjoyed the company, part of him wasn't eager to have to share things, even small things, all the time.

Breakfast was a tense affair, made easier by Georgie's babbling and antics. Mack found himself saying a prayer of thanks for the child's innocence as he walked to the shack that was still serving as the first general store. The trouble with moving the General Store to its new, expanded location was that he could never afford the luxury of closing during the move. People needed everything, all the time, and Mack's was the only decent place to get provisions.

"Everything okay?" Mack called to Danny Whitehorse, the young Tlingit man who served as store clerk, who was already putting out new stock for the day on makeshift shelves and boxes. Mack ducked behind the shack's open front to the small stockroom in the back. He took a moment to scan the ledgers, checked a few crates of incoming supplies and then filled a small box with a pen, writing paper and a collection of other supplies. Mack usually spent Saturday mornings at home preparing his sermon for the following day, but he needed more privacy than home allowed this morning. As such, the church would become his "study" for the day. The sermon wouldn't take long—it was already well settled in his mind, thanks to the sleepless night. It was his other project that demanded peace and quiet.

Chapter Nine

Lana was grateful for the quiet Saturday morning in the cabin. She gave Georgie a bath, took some meat out of the icebox in the cabin floor for dinner—the Alaskan ground, which never really thawed, made keeping food amazingly easy and convenient up here—and set about scrubbing a nasty stain on the cabin floor she'd noticed earlier. It looked like the greasy black spot had been there for years instead of the few months she knew Mack's cabin had stood. "That's what happens when you let things go," she told Georgie as she scraped at the thing with a knife. "Always solve a problem before it becomes a bigger one, Georgie. That's what your grandfather used to say."

Georgie replied by using one of his new blocks to scrape the spot of floor he was sitting on, mimicking her. When she grunted, he did. The imitation made her laugh in spite of her frail mood.

She'd just removed the last of the spot when Mack

returned from his morning errands, or wherever it was that he went. She had no right to be bothered by the fact that he hadn't given her details, only an "I'll be gone," but Jed had always spent hours and hours outlining his plans and schemes to her. Lana found it sadly ironic that she knew Jed's schedule every day, but never knew how badly he'd managed their affairs. Sitting up from her spot hunched over the stain, she blew a lock of hair from her forehead and asked, "Mack Tanner, whatever hit this floor?"

"Tar," he said calmly. "Never did come out."

"Till now. Did you scrub this? Ever?"

His silence convicted him of the crime. "Who knows what else I'll find if I look under the rugs in this place?"

He seemed to wince at the remark, as if it had been the worst thing to say. Come to think of it, he had the look of a man with a lot to say. A furrowed, reluctant brow. He was going to make them talk about the brooches, she knew it. She wasn't ready for that. Things were still jumbled in her chest and she didn't want him to see her cry.

"I don't rightly know how to do this, but God's been after me all morning." He pulled out a chair at their table for her. "Can we talk?"

Lana smoothed her skirt and sat down. Mack folded his hands in the manner of a man about to have a serious conversation. Lana swallowed and tucked her hands onto her lap.

"I'm a man of privacy, Lana. Too many folks

up here would snap up any bit of information they thought was useful, and use it no matter who it harmed. And you know as well as I that most people up here can't be trusted. Not all, but most."

"I am not 'most folks.'"

He paused before answering. "I know that. It's just…well, much as I think the less you know the better, God won't seem to let me alone about the fact that you do deserve to know *some* things. I realize Jed's made that a bit of a sore spot for you, having kept things from you."

It was a sore spot, all right. "Yes. I don't deserve to be kept in the dark, Mack. Least of all by you."

"I suppose that's true. But, I'm a man used to keeping things to myself."

Lana could almost manage a smile. Keeping things to himself was an understatement. Mack Turner was the most private man she had ever known. The man was like Atlas, trying to hoist the world on his solitary shoulders. He'd aged five years in the last two months, from the look of him. Hadn't they both? "I suppose life's handed you good reasons not to trust," she admitted, surprising even herself with the sudden bit of sympathy.

"That's not an excuse for not trusting…my wife," he said it as if God had spent the morning pounding it into his head with a thunderbolt. A reluctant realization. She knew a thing or two about those. "So, like I told you, I've got a plan about what to do with anyone who decides to follow in Jameson's and Nicky Peacock's footsteps."

Lana brought her hands up to the table. "And you've decided to tell me about it?"

"I figure it's best you know. Given what's happened and all."

That was a huge admission for him, and she knew it. She realized right then how much effort this marriage required of him. Under normal circumstances, love would have compelled a loner like Mack Tanner to share with someone else, to be a true life partner. In their situation, Mack was forced to do it without the pull of love. She'd been wrong thinking she'd be the one to have to do all the adapting in this marriage. He was trying to be a true husband to her. The fact that it took such an effort for him tugged at a corner of her heart far more than she wanted to admit. "Thank you," Lana said, hoping the words did her thoughts justice.

That seemed to give him the toehold he needed to press on. He pulled a piece of folded paper from a pocket and placed it on the table. "The way I see it, folks will keep looking for my gold…your gold… *our* gold, whether we want them to or not."

She laughed at the irony of that. The truth was, she'd brought no gold to this marriage, save what was left in her jewelry box. Folks thought otherwise of course, assuming they'd now combined their considerable wealth. He was right about one thing, though: their married financial state posed as many problems as it solved.

"Gold is why they're up here. And if they can't find their own, they're quick to go looking for mine. Or anyone else's for that matter. And the bankers? They can't be trusted at all—you've already seen that. I refuse to put my gold in the bank, which means how I protect my gold is on my own shoulders."

"How *we* protect the gold is on *our* shoulders."

He nodded almost imperceptibly. "I figure the best way to keep them from hunting for mine is to give them another target. A distraction. Other gold to find."

"Whose?"

Mack put his hand into his coat pocket and brought out six sizable gold nuggets. Gold was mostly found in dust from around these parts, and nuggets were prized property. These were large, too. Lana guessed most of the men up on the pass would see the gold in front of her as a fortune worth hunting down.

"No one really cares whose gold this is," he said. "That's the thing of it. I'll hide this somewhere just outside of Treasure Creek, drop a few carefully crafted clues about a new mystery treasure into the rumor mill, and suddenly everyone's looking for this instead of bothering you. There's enough here to throw even Jameson off your trail."

There was. A man could live well for a year on

what Mack laid in front of her. "A decoy treasure." She couldn't help but ask the question. "Can you spare this?"

His face grew serious before he answered. "I could spare three times this, easily." So he *was* as wealthy as everyone suspected. He'd been a wealthy man even before striking the gold he found with Jed. And unlike Jed, he'd kept most of their claim rather than lavishly spending it. Lana guessed Mack had never told anyone the extent of his fortune. There were rumors everywhere about how well-off Mack was, but even Jed had never offered specifics. It struck her that this was as close to an admission of his wealth as Mack ever gave anyone. The realization must have showed on her face, for Mack added in earnest, "You and Georgie will never want for anything, Lana, ever again. I promise you that. And if it took ten times this to buy the safety of my family, I'd do it."

There it was again, that declaration of protection that seemed to cut straight to the center of her heart. It wasn't a flashy, dashing affection—the kind Jed had offered—but it hinted at something deep and trustworthy. How long had it been since she felt she could rely on another human being? Felt taken care of? She stuffed the ambush of emotion back down into the dark corner of her chest where she kept her grief, and resumed the conversation.

"How will you do this?"

"There's a spot back by the waterfall where the

Indians used to hide food. A deep hole shaped like a diamond. Hard to see in winter, but visible now, if you know where to look."

"Sounds like something out of a storybook."

"Exactly. Just hard enough to present a challenge—this can't look too easy—but not so hidden that folks can't figure it out. I figure it'll take them all summer. Buy me some time to get a little more authority in place around here—morally and legally. This town needs a preacher and a sheriff as fast as God and I can manage it."

He still hadn't explained the folded paper. "What's that?"

"That," Mack said slowly, "is for you and Georgie. If anything should ever happen to me, I want you both provided for." He took in a deep breath, as if steeling himself to say the words. "It's a map to where the rest is."

The rest. As in Mack's true fortune. The weight of the information pressed onto her shoulders, heavy as a yoke. "I'll hide the map somewhere on the property. I haven't worked that bit out yet."

Some part of her knew that wasn't the whole truth. He had worked it out—Mack never did anything without having it completely worked out in advance—he just couldn't bring himself to tell her everything. Yet.

But he *had* told her some—it would be unfair to discount that. After all she'd heard today, could she really fault him for not shedding years of mistrust all at once? Mack didn't trust her fully, and that hurt, but Mack trusted no one fully. And the few he had trusted—his brothers, Jed and goodness knows who else—were dead from their foolishness. No, the world had schooled Mack Tanner well in the value of secrecy, and new skills took time to learn. He was trying—hard—and the least she could do was keep an open mind and be patient. They were both learning how to do this, after all.

"You'll work out the best place for it," she said. "For what it's worth, I think it's a very clever plan."

Mack took the map, still folded, and slipped it inside his shirt. "You'll need more wood tonight. It's looking cold. I'll go fetch some from the pile."

Lana realized, after he left, that they'd never once discussed the brooch he'd given her.

Three days later, Lana stood before her first Tuesday morning class and willed her knees not to fail. Mack's Sunday announcement about the "trial" school classes had been impressive. Despite the resistance he held for her role as teacher, Mack had made a strong plea for students. She valued that.

She was staring at the result of that plea right now—ten eager faces, most of whom has been signed up within hours of Mack's announcement in church. Treasure Creek families were indeed eager to get an education for their children. It would have been a lost opportunity to wait until fall. However ill equipped she felt at the present moment, starting now had been the right choice. Especially when one of her students' parents was so grateful for the classes she'd offered to watch Georgie—something Lana had not yet figured out how to solve.

Some students she had expected, others were surprises, but none more so than Leo Johnson, Caleb Johnson's son. Leo sat nervously in the last church pew, looking like a giant compared to the collection of younger students. While most ranged in ages from eight to fourteen, Lana suspected Leo was closer to eighteen—old enough to be up on the trail with the other stampeders, if it weren't for his slow nature. The Ladies' Aid Society back in Seattle often raised charity funds for what were called "the feebleminded," but the term didn't fit Leo at all. He could think, reason and follow directions, but facts came together like molasses in his head. As if his thoughts were stuck in mud.

"Leo wants to learn. Badly," Caleb had said with downcast eyes, as if asking a tremendous favor. "He's frustrated lately. I reckon he needs a challenge, wants to prove himself. I know it takes him longer than most, but he can learn. More than you think, I know it."

Lana's heart twisted at the father's plea. What parent didn't want every possible opportunity for their child? Desire to learn was half the battle anyhow, and Leo had that in abundance.

Indeed, Leo hadn't stopped talking to Mack since the minute church let out. But true to Leo's intellect, he hadn't yet worked out that it was *Lana* who'd teach him, and that Mack had only announced the start of the trial classes. The other children hadn't any issue with his presence—Leo often played with the town children when he wasn't helping Caleb on the docks.

Lana took a deep breath and began her teaching career. "Good morning, I'm Mrs. Tanner, and I'll be your teacher. We're going to sit in special groups by what you can do now," Lana began, "and things will shift as we learn. Now, I've put a list of words on the board." She pointed to the list of successively harder words she'd written on the chalkboard Mack had set up behind her. "Look at these words and count how many you can read."

"One, two…" Leo started, ticking off his fingers.

"Silently," Lana added. "But you can use your fingers if it helps."

It took the better part of an hour to work through the four lists she'd prepared, but by the end of the first class she had the students grouped by reading and mathematical abilities. Betsy Landown, it turned out, could read exceptionally well. Little Matthew Powers couldn't get farther than ABC. Four others barely knew their alphabet, but the majority of the class had basic, if not strong, reading skills. And true to his surprising nature, Leo

Johnson was actually quite good with numbers. It was as if a maze of challenges spread itself before her, an enticing collection of minds, like puzzles to be solved. Lana felt splendidly useful. As if some part of her soul had woken up from a long sleep.

Perhaps the future hadn't been stolen from her after all.

Chapter Ten

"Leo Johnson can add double numbers, did you know that?" Lana was full to bursting to share with Mack all she'd learned about her class. She'd barely eaten a bite of lunch in her eagerness. When was the last time she'd felt this excited about anything?

"You don't say?" he replied just a bit wearily, as he got up to fetch the jar of mustard. In her buzz to tell him everything, she'd forgotten to set it out. Well, the mustard and half a dozen other things. She'd left a handkerchief on her "desk," and she never left handkerchiefs anywhere, ever. She was thankful he hadn't yet mentioned she'd completely forgotten to make breakfast in her rush to get to the classroom ready.

Lana stopped, squinting her eyes shut. "I told you that already, didn't I?"

"Twice," Mack admitted, opening the mustard, "but it is an amazing thing when you think about it. He has a dark temper at times, Lana, so tread carefully. But if you can unlock the puzzle of that mind he's got, who knows what could happen."

Lana sat down opposite him, setting a plate of ham bits before Georgie, who was currently pulling at Mack's hand that held the mustard. "They're all amazing. Each one of them has strengths and weaknesses. If I can figure out how to fit them all together like a puzzle, they'll eventually help each other."

Mack made no reply, save to dab a little mustard on his finger. Before Lana could tell him to stop, Mack indulged Georgie's curiosity. Her son's face twisted up in horror at the sharp taste, sticking his tongue out with a wail.

"Really, Mack," Lana scolded over Georgie's protestations, ducking up to get the cup of milk she'd forgotten on the sideboard.

"Well, I doubt he'll ask for it again. Sometimes the best way to solve a pest is to give them what they think they want. Not that Georgie's a pest, mind you—" he paused and raised an eyebrow at her "—but he has his mother's persistence."

His teasing came more and more frequently, and she liked the warmth of the new Mack. She soothed Georgie's sour face with a bit of apple and leaned on the table with one elbow. "And *your* morning?"

"The outfitting post is busier than ever. The new General Store ought to be ready soon. We got the shelves up against the west walls, and I had enough time to stop in at the barber's and the docks to drop a few important hints, but I still have a pile of ledgers to work my way through this afternoon."

Just the opportunity she was hoping for. "Would you mind going over those ledgers here in the cabin while Georgie naps? I want to go to Viola Goddard's." Viola was a new woman in town, a quiet woman who kept to herself despite Lana's several attempts to make conversation. What excited Lana most was Viola's profession; it was delightful to have a real seamstress in town. Lana planned to support Viola by giving her all the business she could, plus muster up all kinds of work from the other women in town. Not that she was being judgmental, but Treasure Creek's collective wardrobe left much to be desired. Viola's skills were just the ticket, not to mention all the lovely things she could do to make the church and classroom more civilized and comfortable.

"Viola Goddard?" Mack looked suspicious. "Didn't we just buy clothes?"

Lana drew herself up straight. "As it happens, I'm going to talk to Viola about having curtains made for the schoolhouse."

Mack glanced around their home, as if measuring her decorating enthusiasm to see how far she would go on behalf of the classroom. "The schoolhouse won't be done for another month at least."

There's a man for you, Lana scowled. Always underestimating how much time good craftsmanship will take. She wanted to select colors carefully, to plan ahead and think things through. Surely Mack could understand that, planner that he was. She could see him weigh the consequences of refusing now, literally watch him decide to humor her decorating plans. Still, she was a bit surprised when he agreed without an argument. But he didn't let it go without the dangerous question, "Won't the Tucker sisters tend to that?"

Goodness, where was Mack's sense, even considering handing such a task to the likes of the Tuckers? Lana couldn't begin to imagine what those three would dream up, given the task of decorating the schoolhouse. *We'd end up with burlap curtains,* Lana thought to herself as she snatched Mack's lunch plate out from underneath him and tended to the dishes.

A whopping yawn from Georgie called Lana to pluck him from his highchair and ready him for a nap. "You sleep good for your mama now," Mack called, as Georgie waved to him over her shoulder. He'd be out like a light in no time, leaving Mack in peace to work and her a good stretch of time to make plans with Viola.

She walked out into the sunlight, again marveling at the crispness of the summer air. Lana was stopped no less than six times over the short walk to the cabin that served as Viola's shop and home, each stop by someone needing something from Mack. Or unloading a complaint. Or even downright griping.

Lana was quickly learning that being Mrs. Treasure Creek meant one got nowhere fast or alone.

"I'll be happy to pass that along to Mack, Mr. Burns," Lana said as she knocked on Viola's door. "I'm sure he'll be very interested to hear your views." As soon as Viola opened the door even an inch, Lana ducked inside and shut it behind her. She sighed as Viola raised an eyebrow. "There seems to be no shortage of opinions in this town."

Viola gave her an odd look. "What can I do for you, Mrs. Tanner?"

"Lana, please." She cocked her head in the direction of the street. "I've had just about enough of being Mrs. Tanner for the moment."

"Lana, then. And please call me Viola. Now, how can I help you?" Viola was a lovely woman with striking red hair and soft eyes. She had the look of a woman who'd been through some difficulties, but she never took Lana up on any questions about her life before Treasure Creek. It wasn't that odd a trait; lots of folks in Treasure Creek were leaving unpleasantness behind them, but the wistful quality behind Viola's eyes often made Lana wonder just what the woman had left back in… Lana realized Viola had never told anyone where she was from. Her privacy couldn't be held against her. Keeping to oneself in a place as small and boisterous as Treasure Creek was no small endeavor, she knew that from wanting to crawl from view just after Jed died. It made her sad to sense the same "leave me to myself" attitude in Viola's minimal talk and defiant eyes.

"Viola, you can help me a great deal. I want you to help me create wonderful things for the schoolhouse. Bright colors, fabrics that will hold up, that sort of thing. I want our schoolhouse to be outfitted with care and quality, and I gather you're just the woman for the job."

"I'm so glad," Viola offered, a smile breaking across her face. "When I heard you were teaching, I dearly hoped you'd be the one to decorate the schoolhouse when it was finished."

"Really?" She could see in Viola's eyes what she was going to say next, and it made Lana sure she'd just made a new ally.

"Well, I have to say," Viola ventured carefully, "I wasn't at all sure how picking out fabrics with the Tucker sisters would go."

Lana laughed. "If they picked out any fabrics at all. I suspect, if they had final say, Treasure Creek's students would be learning surrounded by flannel and denim, if not on bare wood. I want our classroom to be wonderfully decorated, and I want you to take it on. Will you?"

"I'd be delighted. I can go over and take measurements tomorrow if you like."

Lana reached into her reticule. "I've already brought the measurements with me."

"Well, then," Viola smiled, "I've just made some

tea, perhaps we can sit down and go over your ideas together."

This was just the result Lana was hoping for. "I have so many ideas. And not just about the school." Lana walked over to the little table Viola had set up in the charmingly decorated kitchen. Like Lana, with not too many resources Viola had done much to make a home. "Believe me, Viola, I have all kinds of ideas for Treasure Creek that I think you'll find very interesting—and should bring you lots of business, besides."

Mack tallied up the May store ledgers, but his mind kept wandering to how Lana had looked when she left. She had a smart jacket over her shirtwaist, and a hat pinned to her piles of yellow curls, but he mostly noticed how she wore a lace scarf tied where the brooch used to go. Yes, she'd worn his brooch to church on Sunday, but some prideful part of him took note that, while she'd worn Jed's pin daily, she did not keep his gift so close. He was ashamed of the reaction, thinking himself petty and spiteful, but even multiple discussions of it with God had failed to squelch the dark response.

Once he was sure enough time had passed for Georgie to be soundly asleep, Mack made his way into her room, to the small pine box where he knew Lana kept her jewelry. He removed both brooches, bringing them to his desk where the map he'd discussed with Lana but not shown her lay unfolded.

The map outlined a crude stretch of the Chilkoot Trail and its relation to Treasure Creek. Surrounded by rough approximations of landmarks and several complicated calculations of paces in various directions, lay a bright red "X", marking Mack's cache of gold. As such, Mack's desk now held the most valuable piece of paper in Treasure Creek, maybe even this part of Alaska—but only if the bearer had the key needed to read the map.

As extra protection, the map was intentionally missing a compass key, stating which direction was north in the drawing. Mack had gone to great trouble to draw the map vague enough as to be useless without a key. Now for the final touch: using the two pins, Mack drew a colored key that looked like the pin he'd given Lana, but in reality used the skewed alignments of the colored stones in the now-bent pin Jed had given her. Lana's new pin looked distinctly like compass points, but only Jed's pin would render the map useful. It was a brilliant plan. Although it had come to him after he'd had Lana's pin made, it couldn't have been more perfect if he'd planned it out in advance.

Smiling at the perfection of it all, Mack leaned back and tested his design one final time. Yes, if he laid Lana's new pin over the compass key and lined up the colored stones, it clearly looked like one side of the map was north. If he put Jed's pin over the key and lined up the colors, however, it revealed that north on this map was actually diagonally off to the left. Using the new pin would throw any robber way off-track, sending him counting paces in directions that would never lead him to Mack's fortune. It was the perfect secret key; she'd never throw the old pin away, but she'd never wear it. If she ever chose to wear his pin more than on Sundays—and some part of him hoped that would be true someday—it would only strengthen the deception.

She'd been hurt that he wouldn't trust her with the map's location. Now he could tell her where the map would be hidden on his property and still be protected. She knew half of what she needed, and someday, he'd tell her the whole of it. He'd promised to provide for her and Georgie, after all. But at least now, if something happened to him, he could send word back to her about the pin, and only she would understand. Not a flawless plan, for he hadn't yet worked out what would happen if he died and couldn't send word back about the pin key. Well, he simply couldn't die. It was the best he could do for now.

Mack quietly placed the jewelry box back onto Lana's bureau beside a still sleeping Georgie. Yes, it was the best he could do for now.

"Six times on my way to Viola Goddard's!" she declared as she opened the cabin door to find Mack bent over a stack of ledgers with Georgie banging blocks at his feet. "I was stopped six times. And twice as many on my way *from* her shop. How do you stand it?"

Mack straightened up, folding the ledger closed. "I thought you liked being the center of attention." It was the closest thing to teasing she'd heard from him yet. She hadn't really thought Mack Tanner capable of having a twinkle in his eye, but his smiles toward her had definitely warmed.

"Depends on the kind," she replied, taking off her bonnet and hanging it next to his hat on the pegs by the door. "And, I suppose, the subject matter. What ever did you say, and to whom, to get folks so worked up over this treasure business?"

Mack crossed his hands over his chest, clearly pleased with how his plan had unfolded. "Let's just say it's useful to know which ears lead to which mouths."

"A Russian czar's gold? Really?"

"No, but the Russians were the first here. They cared more about furs than gold. America bought Alaska from the Russian government. The most effective rumors have to have a grain of truth in them."

Lana set down the swatches of material she and Viola had settled on on the table. Together they'd chosen summer and winter curtains for the school, as well as some seat cushions for the benches and chairs. Students would learn far better if they weren't forced to sit on cold, hard chairs when winter came. She loved creating the right environment for learning, weaving all the details together to achieve an outcome. It satisfied some internal appetite she didn't even know she had. It'd be a while before these ideas came to fruition, before the actual curtains were hung in the actual school, but even talking about ideas for designs gave her an energy she thought she'd lost forever. "Blue and gold," she said, as she watched Mack's eyes wander over the half-dozen squares of cloth. "Blue for the sky…"

"And gold for Alaska's favorite obsession?"

"I prefer to think of it as her most valuable resource."

Mack laughed. "I'd argue Alaska's most valuable resource is the sheer spunk of the folks who make it up here."

Lana sat down. "Spunk? Folks here are relentless. Do I know if there are really only six nuggets? Did I hear one of them was the size of a man's fist?" She eyed Mack. "Did someone really take apart the pulpit, thinking it was in the base?" The church didn't even have a real pulpit; Mack had ordered one from Seattle, but he preached from an adapted rolltop desk until its arrival. Someone speculated the desk drawers had been nailed shut with the gold nuggets inside. Honestly, the stories grew wilder every day.

"No. But someone dug three different holes in the churchyard last night. And Caleb told me someone pulled up the boards on two different docks."

Georgie left his place at Mack's feet to climb

up on Lana's lap and pick up two of the swatches. Some days it was such a pleasure to watch him play with even the simplest of things. She hadn't realized how much the day-to-day struggle for survival had stolen her joy. "Just as long as no one starts digging around here." Struck by the idea, she asked, "Is that why you started the bit about the Russian czar? So no one would suspect you?"

"I didn't start the bit about the Russian czar."

"But you…" The man had secrecy down to an art form.

"I only said it was a valid rumor. I didn't say I started it."

Lana let her head fall into one hand. The whole thing seemed one large tangle. "It makes me wonder, Mack Tanner, how you keep the difference between truth and rumor straight in that head of yours. A man who starts to believe his own schemes is on the road to trouble."

Mack's eyes darkened over, and Lana realized her remark came out as more of an accusation than she would have liked. Yes, she thought he was playing a dangerous game, but he hadn't ever proven himself untrustworthy. "I know what I'm doing," he said seriously. "You can trust me."

What an odd thing for such an untrusting man to say. "If you want to be trusted, you have to do some trusting yourself." How had she become so bold with him?

"I know that."

"Do you?"

Mack stared at her for a moment, and she could see a decision forming behind his eyes. "I have something to show you," he said, the words stiff and forced.

Lana nodded, hesitant to say anything.

He pulled out the folded paper she recognized from earlier, but left it still folded. "You're my wife. You and Georgie are my responsibility now. There are things I suppose you should know, things you may need to know…someday."

She waited for him to venture further information.

"This is the map to where my gold is, Lana. It'll be…" He actually hesitated. It really was difficult for him to share this information, and while his secrecy agitated her, she could at least appreciate the effort this seem to cost him. "It will be buried in a tin box under the southwest fence post of the garden in back. That's all you'll ever need to know while…while I'm here."

The unspoken, "unless I die and leave you a widow twice over" hung in the air between them, thick as suspicion.

Lana didn't know how to respond. He clearly didn't trust her. Not completely. Yet her intuition told her he wasn't capable of trusting her completely. At least not now. Still, it hurt to know he kept things from her. The deep wounds of Jed's deception left scars too big for it not to hurt. Lana managed a "thank you," but she suspected it sounded too much like the reply she'd given at his gift of the brooch. She should be more gracious at his effort, but she couldn't. Why must everything be such a double-edged sword between them? What a sad pair they made. Every attempt Mack made at healing their wounds only served to open them back up again.

He never unfolded the map to show it to her. She didn't ask to see it.

After a moment, he slipped it back into his pocket. She knew that after Mack returned from his walk tonight, when the sun finally surrendered the sky, she would hear him shoveling in the backyard, burying this map they would probably never speak of again.

Chapter Eleven

Town meetings in Treasure Creek happened once a month. That was probably as often as the residents could stand. Mack couldn't remember a single one that hadn't ended in some kind of argument. With all the treasure-hunting ruckus of the past week, Mack said a prayer for peace twice over, as folks filed into the church pews.

The first "town meeting," held around a fire in the cluster of tents that had been Treasure Creek's earliest settlement, had also been its first fight. Over this very church. From the moment God had called him to build this town, Mack knew its church must be the first true building to be raised in Treasure Creek. It had to be right in the center of town, had to be the first four walls to go up anywhere on the settlement. "A symbol," Mack had proclaimed, "of who we are and what we stand for."

Not everyone thought that so fine an idea. Lana, as a matter of fact, found it particularly hard to swallow. Tent walls were thin, and more than once he'd heard her sharp words to Jed about "not waiting in line behind God's house for a house of her own." Granted, March evenings were cold, and he couldn't much blame her when twice she took Georgie "back to Skaguay to sleep within solid walls."

It always surprised him that Jed had never once questioned his decision. While he would have liked to say Jed shared his faith and vision for Treasure Creek, it was sadly more accurate to say that Jed lacked the spine to disagree. Jed never shared Mack's values as much as he merely surrendered to them. Still, there was something about Jed that made him a fine friend despite his many weaknesses. Mack missed him every single day, just as he missed his brothers who had joined Jed and the thousands of other men who lost their lives up on the Chilkoot Trail.

First order of town meeting business was always the welcome of new residents. Viola Goddard received her formal welcome, as did two families with new babies, two couples and five bachelors. A total of ten new "households" were formally added to the community tonight, each of them drawn to the God-centered values this little church declared. At the rate things were going, Treasure Creek would hit five hundred residents next month, and easily a thousand by the end of the year, if not the end of the season.

Mack was about to move on to the next order of

business when Margie Tucker stood. "In relation to those new folks here," she began, when Mack recognized her to speak, "we've been discussing a proposition."

The other Tucker sisters, not to mention about a dozen other people throughout the room, nodded in agreement. There wasn't much that went on in Treasure Creek without Mack's knowing about it, so this struck him as distinctly odd. And a bit unnerving.

"We think Treasure Creek needs a mayor. And every single one of us thinks it ought to be you. You do everything else around here, it can't hurt to just make it official."

"Mayor?" Mack stepped back a bit from his place behind the pulpit, genuinely surprised. He'd expected the residents of Treasure Creek to resist any further formalization of the town, not instigate it.

"Sounds a whole lot better than 'Mr. Treasure Creek,' don't you think?" Margie said, wiggling her fingers at the crowd to elicit cries of agreement.

"I expect we could add a town council, eventually," Ed Parker offered. "We're getting big enough to need one." He looked back at the row of folks standing in the back of the room. "We barely fit in here as it is."

"There will always be room for every person in Treasure Creek to come inside this church," Mack said, meaning it. "Even if we have to build out every two months to fit them in." He gestured to the newly expanded sanctuary foundation already underway. It hadn't been the first church construction effort, and it wouldn't be the last.

"You best build fast," Caleb Johnson replied. "There's three more big ships docking this week alone. Which means we'll keep getting more people, which means we need a mayor."

Mack wiped his hands down his face. He'd always thought of himself more as a "founding father" than a politician, but Margie had a point; being declared mayor wouldn't change his day-to-day existence much—folks came to him for everything as it was. "Don't mayors have to be elected?"

Margie planted her hands on her hips. "Well, now I figured that'd just be a formality. All in favor of making Mack Tanner mayor, say 'aye.'"

In Treasure Creek's first—and perhaps only— act of total agreement, the entire room erupted in "aye."

"What if someone else wants to run?" Mack felt obligated to point out. Weren't elections generally involving a *choice* of candidates? This was feeling a bit like a spontaneous coronation.

Margie's answer to that question was to level a glare of defiance around the room. "Anyone else want to run against Mack?" The way she put it, it wasn't a real question at all. More like a "raise your hand and I'll wallop you," without words. Unsurprisingly, silence filled the room.

Duncan MacDougal stood and cleared his throat.

"I move we elect Mack Tanner Mayor of Treasure Creek." He sounded terribly official, as if he would record it on some tablet somewhere, the moment the deed was done. As it was, Lucy Tucker, who acted as secretary to the town meetings because she'd learned shorthand somewhere along her many adventures, was already bent over her papers scribbling furiously. "All in favor…"

"I already did that," Margie interrupted.

"You needed a motion." Duncan sounded put out. "And a motion must always be seconded."

"I should think *you* just seconded the idea I had *first*." Margie did not care to be second on anything. Mack thought he was watching Treasure Creek's one and only "unanimous" go up in smoke over a procedural formality.

"Just second MacDougal and be done with it," snapped Hattie Marsh, one of the older residents in Treasure Creek. Hattie's husband nodded in mutual frustration. Miners weren't sticklers for procedure, that was clear.

Evidently, Tuckers were. "I was first," Margie protested.

"It doesn't matter." Ed Parker stood up to his full height, giving him almost two feet over feisty little Margie Tucker.

"I suppose not," Margie acquiesced. And not half a minute later, Mack Tanner became Mayor Tanner.

The warmth and width of Mrs. Tanner's smile didn't escape Mack's notice.

They walked home an hour later, Georgie fast asleep on Mack's shoulder. There was something comforting about the warm weight of the little boy, even if he was soaking through the shoulder of Mack's shirt as he sucked his thumb. He'd been right about the effect families would have on the men up here. Men often got wild up on the trail— one only had to float the ten miles downriver to Skaguay to see how civilized men could combine liquor and money into a dangerous brew. Adding women to the mix often did as much harm as it did good. But families—mothers, fathers, sisters, brothers, grandparents, aunts and uncles—those things grounded a man, made him think beyond his next diversion.

Already, the man he'd been had changed because Georgie and Lana were in the picture. Thinking past himself for the sake of Treasure Creek, that hadn't been much of a stretch for a natural-born leader like Mack. Thinking past himself for the sake of his *family*—that had pushed him too far already. Lana had begun to figure into his decisions, and far too many of this thoughts. He'd come to draw a surprising comfort from the sounds and scents of her in his house. In *their* home. There was no denying it, Lana had made his house a home. Walking to that home, feeling the boy's head settled into the crook of his neck, feeling the rise and fall of that little chest against his collarbone, an assurance settled into Mack; Treasure Creek had been the right thing to do. It was worth any battle, worth doing whatever it took. Even if it took becoming mayor.

"Welcome home, Your Honor," Lana said, as she lifted the latch on their cabin. She dropped a comical little curtsey as she stepped inside.

"I don't know what they think having a mayor will do." He angled himself and Georgie through the door, holding Georgie off him just enough for Lana to get the boy's coat off. "They won't argue any less."

"They'll just rely on you more." Lana cocked her head to one side. "You know that."

"I've no illusions my life just got easier, that's for certain." Mack turned Georgie over in his arms so that he cradled him now, letting Lana unlace her son's boots and tug them gently off. It still amazed him that Georgie could be such a crazy little monkey while awake, and yet look so sweetly peaceful when asleep. He'd been a noisy, fidgety distraction during half the town meeting, before finally conking out. "I suppose you'll need to do a lesson on government this week, now that you're the mayor's wife."

"We're learning science lessons tomorrow," Lana said with no small amount of pride, as she opened the door that led into her and Georgie's room. "Metals, to be precise. I thought it a relevant subject." He angled past her, brushing close to all her soft scents as he did so. Glory, but that woman smelled wonderful all the time.

"Metals?" Mack grinned as he laid the boy down. Georgie, who always seemed to take forever to fall asleep but thankfully slept like a rock once out, made a small mumbling sound and snuggled in. Lana's "proud mama" smile beamed as she pulled the quilt up over his round little body.

"Iron, tin, silver and, of course, gold."

The next morning, four objects sat on Lana's classroom desk. Things they'd all seen, things some of the students used every day, but each representing the four metals she'd chosen to teach. "Iron is used in many everyday objects, mostly for its strength, durability and price." She wrote "IRON" in large letters on the slate behind her, then held up the horseshoe she'd borrowed from Duncan yesterday. "We get iron ore out of the ground and make things with it. Who can tell me who does this for us in Treasure Creek?"

"Mr. MacDougal," one girl blurted out with enthusiasm.

She did the same process with the three other objects, knowing full well most of her students were waiting for her to display the last item. "The final metal we'll be studying today has particular meaning to our town. It's precious, very pretty, but not as practical as our other metals, for a variety of reasons."

"Everybody wants it," a student said from the front row.

Men die for it, Lana thought silently as she wrote "GOLD" on the slate. She banished the thought's shadow from her countenance as she turned to face the class again. "So, everyone, who can tell me why are our plates are made from tin but our pins made from gold?"

While the variety of answers was entertaining and inventive, none of them were the fact she was looking for. "Gold is too soft for many practical uses." She wrote the word "SOFT" beside "GOLD"—the class was most competent at words between three and five letters, which is why she'd chosen gold, silver, tin and iron as their subject matter. She held up the dented pin Jed had given her. "Georgie is just a little boy, and he was able to do this damage."

"That's sad." Leo's deep voice rang through the room. "It was pretty before."

The rest of the class time was so energized and effective, Lana was bursting with pride. The attention her students gave to the lesson confirmed her hunch—reading and spelling went much better when the subject matter was of interest. Lists of words, even with pictures next to them, failed to garner much enthusiasm with this crowd. The conversations and effort they put into reading today's words made Lana beam with satisfaction as she dismissed class for the day. She was good at this. She should be tired, but Lana hummed in high spirits to herself as she returned books to their shelves and wiped off the slate.

Until she looked at her desk.

"I can't believe it's gone!" Lana was near tears as Mack rushed to the church with her.

"You're sure?" Mack pushed open both doors of the church to let as much sunlight into the sanctuary as possible.

"I've gone over every inch of the room—twice— and it's not there. I can't have lost it. I should never have used it in the first place."

Mack had entertained that thought, knowing it was the key to the map he'd drawn for her. He'd been annoyed—angry even—that she'd suddenly pulled it out of her hiding place and planned to take it out to school, of all places. Still, it wasn't as if he could forbid her to do so. He surely couldn't tell her why her old pin was so valuable.

Mack surveyed Lana's desk, a table set up in the front of the pews that served as the makeshift class-room. Each of the three other objects were still lined up on the desk in perfect order. He didn't like the conclusion forming in his mind. Lana would like it even less. "Where were you standing when you dismissed the class?"

Lana pointed to a back pew. "Over here, helping Jenny Wilson make a proper letter 'G'."

Across the room, with her back turned to the desk. Mack pinched the bridge of his nose, hating what he had to say next. "Lana, someone took the brooch."

"That's not possible. No one was in here but…" Hurt cut so sharply through her features that he felt it behind his ribs. "My students would not steal from me."

This was Alaska, and they'd barely been her students a week. It was highly possible, probable even. He'd seen grown men do worse for less.

"No," she repeated, but even as she declared the single word, he could see her coming to the same inescapable conclusion. And he hated what it did to her eyes. "It's got to have fallen somewhere and I just can't see it. They loved the lesson. Everyone had something to contribute. It was such a good day. And now my precious brooch is gone." She tucked her hand to her mouth to keep from crying.

They spent another ten minutes combing every inch of the sanctuary—Lana's desk, her pockets, even the hem of her skirts in search of the pin, but Mack knew they'd find nothing. He tried to offer some words of comfort, but they sounded hollow and trite. Map key aside, he hated the part of him that was hurt by her loyalty to that pin. She loved Jed. He had no right to resent that love. He'd known exactly what he was getting into when he married her still deep in her grief. He'd known exactly what he was trying to do—and how foolish it was—when he replaced that pin. "I'll find who took it, Lana, and get it back to you," Mack said as he gathered up her shawl and hoisted Georgie on his shoulders. It didn't make up for all his tangled motives, but it was a start.

Lana pulled the church doors shut with a defiant force. "I won't believe a student took it."

That was the trouble with Alaska. People were always believing things in spite of the hard truth in front of them.

Chapter Twelve

Lana and Mack ate lunch in near silence, lost in their own thoughts. Georgie, quick to pick up on tensions, became extra fussy, and she'd had to work hard to get him to go down for an afternoon nap. Mack had left soon after lunch, telling her he was going to the homes of each student to ask questions. He'd promised not to be heavy-handed, but his dark look said otherwise. Bumps in the road were bound to happen as she tried to craft this odd little classroom, but she hadn't expected something so…mean. The act of theft itself felt like such an attack. That it was Jed's brooch just made it all the more painful.

Why, Lord?

The instinctual cry to heaven stopped her. She hadn't even bothered to trouble God with so much as an angry thought since Jed's death. She'd shut that part of her off entirely.

Why are You stealing everything from me? There.

She'd said it. Lana waited for a instant, half expecting a thunderbolt to crash down out of the clouds and smite her for daring to be angry with the Almighty. *Where's the good in this? The higher purpose?*

Georgie whimpered from his room, and she had the startling thought that all had not been taken from her. She had Georgie. And she had the protection Mack offered.

But she'd been driven to the desperation of taking it. *The Lord giveth and the Lord taketh away,* that was the only verse of which she could be certain. Loving kindness, justice, grace, all those things Mack seemed able to see around him? Those felt miles away from anywhere she stood. *Will You take this class from me now, too? Crush me to bits after I've found something that makes me so...happy?*

The earth did not loom up and swallow her whole for railing against God's unfairness to her. As a matter of fact, Lana felt like she'd let loose a stopped-up bottle inside. Uncorked a simmering anger, yet lived to tell the tale. Was yelling at God the same thing as praying?

Lana sank into Mack's chair by the hearth, her hand laying on the black leather Bible he always kept beside it. *I can't see what He sees!* Her spirit seemed to moan the words up out of her chest into the sky. *All I see is loss and pain. Trickery, lies and now...theft. They can't have stolen from me, Lord, and not that. Hasn't life hurt me enough?*

Lana didn't expect some deep voice to declare

His intentions from out of the heavens. She didn't expect God to show His face in high drama right there in front of her. But she did expect something other than the yawning emptiness, the silence of the house that surrounded her so thickly, it pressed against her lungs—as if the anger had evaporated— for now—and left a great sharp-edged void in its place. She could have been standing at the summit of the Chilkoot Pass and not have felt as cold as she did at that moment.

Lana couldn't have said how much time passed until Mack pushed through the cabin door. He had Leo Johnson by one arm, while Leo's father Caleb had a grip on the boy's other elbow. It wasn't really fair to call Leo a boy—he stood head-to-head with Mack, and had a few inches on his own father, he was so large. He was a boy captured in a man's body. A child, really, but with all the strength of a full-grown man. She'd refused to give credence to the tiny voice inside her that suspected Leo was to blame. His hunger to learn despite so many inca-pacities had tugged such affection out of her. Some part of her wanted success for him even more than he wanted it for himself. She wanted to be the one to unlock words for him. It stabbed at her to see him clenched in Mack and Caleb's grip, a man's anger and a boy's guilt warring on his face.

"Leo has something to say to you, Mrs. Tanner," Caleb said, his own face reflecting the heavy disap-pointment Lana felt in her heart.

Leo stood in defiant silence for a moment, then with a prod in the ribs from his father, muttered out, "I took your gold."

Mack produced Jed's brooch from his coat pocket and laid it on the table.

Lana tried to catch his eyes, but he refused to look up.

"Leo, why?"

Mack's expression told her he found that a useless question. She didn't really want to know why he'd stolen, Lana wanted to know why he'd stolen from *her*. It was clear Mack didn't make that distinction.

"It's pretty and I wanted it. Gold's worth lots, even if it is soft and im…impractical."

It stung that he'd so absorbed her lesson but stole from her anyway. "You stole from me, Leo. Something very important to me."

"And he'll pay for his crime," Mack said darkly. "No more school, and four days in jail in Skaguay."

"Away?" Leo asked, looking at his father.

Lana raised an eyebrow to Mack at the severity of the punishment. Did Leo really understand what he'd done? Did Mack understand what a band of Skaguay inmates could do to the likes of someone like Leo? Caleb kept his eyes on the ground, but Lana saw a slight tremble in his shoulders.

"Theft of any kind cannot be tolerated." Mack's

voice was ice and steel. "Not under any circumstances. Not by anyone."

"Must you be so harsh?" Lana said to Mack, after Leo and Caleb had left with instructions to have Leo on the docks to meet the first ferry tomorrow morning.

Mack turned and looked at her. "As a matter of fact, yes. Theft must be severely punished, Lana. Especially up here. Maybe especially in Leo's case."

"Would you have sent young Matty Harris to jail if it were him?"

"I don't know."

She was pleased to see he was at least somewhat bothered by what had just transpired. She found the whole episode heartbreaking and disappointing to say the least. As if a lifetime of damage were unfolding before her and she could do nothing to prevent it. "Leo's mind isn't much different. You know what could happen to him in Skaguay."

Mack broadened his stance. "I know what will happen to him if he steals from someone else. I've watched Leo on the docks. He wants things he can't have. He has a boy's greed but not a man's common sense. He'll never have much money. He has to learn that stealing is dead wrong and has big consequences. There are men up on that trail who would shoot him for what he's done. On the spot, without hesitation. Leo's a *man*, Lana, no matter how slow." He turned from her, slamming his hat down on the peg by the door. "I'm doing him a favor, coming down so hard on him the first time he breaks the law. I'm hoping it means there won't be a next time."

Lana bit back her tongue, but managed a grunt of disagreement despite her reserve.

"Caleb's a friend. Do you think I *like* doing this? People look to me to set standards in Treasure Creek. I've looked the other way too often where Leo is concerned. No more. I've no choice here."

Lana walked to the table and picked up the brooch. Despite Leo's size and strength, it hadn't been further bent at all. He'd been careful with it. He hadn't meant any harm. "He stole from *me*. Don't *I* have a choice?"

"Not in this case." Mack's cold tone left nothing open for discussion. It was like he was another man. Judgmental and almost merciless.

"Jail is bad enough, but to bar him from school? Why don't you just condemn him to never learning at all?" She picked up one of the readers she had stacked on the table. "Leo has a mind, Mack. You should see him with numbers. He's capable of so much more."

"Exactly." Mack pointed at her, his eyes sharp and hard. "It's what he's *capable of* that's the problem here. Lana, I can't trust him in the same room with you. With Georgie. With the other children. I should never have agreed to it in the first place. It's a bad idea. For everyone."

"He made a mistake."

"Which he'll pay for. And hopefully not make another."

Some fearful vulnerability seized Lana's throat, churning up anger and fear. "How many mistakes did Jed make? You managed to forgive him over and—"

"And look what happened!" Mack bellowed, hands flung in the air. "Dead! Lying and stealing just lead to death up here, Lana. There's no room for mercy here. Not for anyone. Not if we want to survive." He gathered his lost temper for a minute, hearing Georgie's wail as the raised voices had awakened him. "Leo stole from you. You only have the brooch back because I went after him. Why on earth are you defending him?"

"Because it's too harsh," Lana hissed in reply as she went toward the bedroom door. "You're a ruthless man, Mack Turner. Will you be a ruthless father to Georgie, too?"

She barely contained herself from slamming the door shut behind her as she went to calm her son. What kind of man had she married?

Every face in the church pews seemed to press Mack down with their expectations as he gave the Sunday lesson. Yesterday had been draining. He'd barely slept after the near-silent dinner spent with

Lana. He was protecting her; he'd gone to great lengths to get her brooch back, and she seemed to take offense at his efforts.

Which bothered him. Immensely. He'd told himself that the brooch must be returned because it was Lana's key to the treasure map, and that was true. But it also burrowed under his skin that Leo had stolen from Lana. She'd poured her heart into teaching him—into teaching all of them—and he repaid her by stealing. He needed to be the law here. And law had to be firm here if Treasure Creek was going to be an upright, respectable community. He'd shut himself off from the fearful look in Leo's eyes as he and Caleb placed him in the custody of the ferry captain for delivery to the sheriff in Skaguay. Lucy Tucker, who seemed to get along especially with Leo, and was friendly with Caleb, stared at him with sharp eyes as she stood with Caleb during the whole painful exchange. The look Caleb gave him as Lucy pulled him away from the dock wrapped a cloak of ice around Mack's heart that had yet to thaw. Had he done the right thing by coming down so hard on Leo? Was there room for mercy in a place like Treasure Creek, surrounded as it was by violence, corruption and deception? Not usually a man to second-guess his decisions, Mack found himself mired in a murky doubt that soured his mood.

Not that there wasn't enough bad news to fuel a bad mood for a week of Saturdays. Ship-docking days were always chaos for his business, but with the old Outfitting Post running half-dismantled and the new General Store not yet open, yesterday had been pandemonium. This new batch of stampeders seemed less prepared than the last. He had fifteen customers for boots and only eight pairs. Trail rations that should have come in on the same boat which carried Leo away failed to arrive, leaving him understocked. And that was just at the Outfitting Post; the list of construction woes at the new General Store was twice as long.

"'Thou shalt not covet thy neighbor's house,'" Mack quoted from the Bible open to *Exodus* on the pulpit before him. "'Thou shalt not covet thy neighbor's wife, nor his manservant, nor his maidservant, nor his ox, nor his donkey, nor any thing that is thy neighbor's.' None of us in Treasure Creek has all he needs. Scarcity will be in our community, and more so when winter comes. But if we can learn to trust God's provision, to be the community He has in mind, I believe we will survive. I believe we will prosper. We must, however, hold close the values we know to be true." He ventured a glance at Lana. "Even when it is hard."

It wasn't as if Lana had never looked at him with a sharp glance before; he'd been on the receiving end of any number of Lana's tirades. It was just that it mattered now. Far more than he liked.

Chapter Thirteen

Church felt odd and out of sorts. Folks came up and congratulated him on his new position as mayor. Lana stood smiling beside him as people filed out of the sanctuary, but where he used to treasure this greeting time, this morning it felt forced and false. *I cannot preach with tension between us.* The verse about making peace with your brother—in this case making peace with his wife—rumbled around in the back of his head as he made small talk with this family and that miner. Caleb, he noted gravely, slipped out without a greeting. "Authority can weigh far more than a man likes," his preacher father had said to him once, when the church had come down hard on one of Mack's childhood buddies. "I must place God's law above the affection of men, even if it costs me that affection." *I don't want to lose Caleb as a friend,* Mack prayed as he shook yet another congratulatory hand. *I've lost enough already.*

The last hand shook, Mack turned to start stacking up the hymnals and such, only to find Viola Goddard standing in the back of the church. She'd been at Sunday services since her arrival only a few weeks ago, and he'd not realized until just this moment that she hadn't been in attendance this morning.

The more surprising thing was that Viola Goddard was holding a baby.

The woman had no child as far as he knew—he'd certainly never seen her with one. Even though the seamstress liked her privacy, Mack was pretty sure he would have seen the child before now. What was going on?

"Mr. Tanner," she said, looking twice over her shoulder. Her voice was tight with worry. "I must speak with you. Right now." Inside a thick blanket, the baby gave out a whimper.

"And who is this?" Lana asked, peering into the folds of cloth.

The new seamstress had not talked of a family, nor was she wearing a wedding ring. As a matter of fact, Viola Goddard had been decidedly stingy with any details of her past. Not that an unspoken desire for "a fresh start" was uncommon up here. Mack had learned to only pry when he deemed it necessary.

The woman offered an unsteady smile. "I don't know."

"What do you mean?"

She met Mack's eyes. "I mean I truly don't know. I found her outside my door in a cradle."

"Abandoned?" Lana's hand went to her chest.

"Yes and no." Viola reached into one corner of the blanket and produced a small sheet of paper. "There was a note."

Mack scanned the neat script.

My brother sent me this gold as proof there's gold up in Dawson's City. It's my only chance to provide for my motherless baby girl. Please take care of her until I can—if I can—make it back home. Use this gold to care for her. I know I can trust you.

There was no signature, nothing to indicate the identity of the child or her parents. Of all the ills and vices he expected to battle in Treasure Creek, he'd never have counted abandoned babies among them. "You don't know who did this?"

"I haven't a clue, Mr. Tanner. But this little girl has been entrusted to me. I'm willing to care for her." Her eyes pleaded with him. "I don't want the gold they left with her. I just want the chance to keep her safe and healthy."

"Gold?" Lana stopped staring at the tot's tiny Indian-style moccasins, to look up at the seamstress.

"They left two nuggets of gold to pay for her care. And a feeding bottle and such. Mr. Tanner, I don't want that gold. I want you to keep it for now. You're in charge here, I felt you ought to know."

He was glad she'd come to him, but stumped as to what to do about the matter. The parents—if that's who truly left the child—had obviously singled Viola Goddard out. He wasn't really in any position to disagree.

"And you truly have no idea who's left this little native girl with you?" Lana voiced his own thoughts. "Or why they'd do such a thing?"

"No, but I'm ready and willing to make sure she's safe and sound."

Lana put her hand on Viola's arm. "Of course you are, Viola. And little..."

"Goldie," she replied, "I just call her Goldie, on account of the nuggets. And on account of these initials on her blanket." Surely enough, the letters "GC" were embroidered on the baby's blanket edging. "There's a 'C' carved on the bottom of the cradle she was left in, too, but I don't know any more than that. The moccasins do make me wonder if she's Tlingit. Her hair is dark enough, but her skin is fair." She rocked the child, holding her close. "But I know she'll be safe with me." She turned to Mack. "I thought you should know, Mr. Tanner. I thought it best to come to you right away."

Mack took the small sack of gold nuggets and the folded sheet of paper. "You were right to, Miss Goddard." He drew his hand across his chin, trying to assess the situation. "I don't rightly know all that's going on with this, but I suspect whoever left little Goldie here with you had good reasons for doing it. So it's best she stays with you until we can figure things out." The seamstress relaxed visibly at this. Did she really expect Mack to yank the child out of her arms? Did people regard him as that harsh? "I expect her father or mother will be back soon, and then we can get to the bottom of this."

"Goodness. However will you feed her? She looks about—oh, I'd say six months or so, wouldn't you?" Lana frowned at the moccasins, with their bold design that clearly marked her as native. "We ought to find you some other baby things."

Viola shifted the baby and rocked slowly from side to side, soothing the child. "Like I said, they left a feeding bottle and some clothing. I can make up anything else she might need in the meantime. I've more than enough fabric, even for diapers. She's a sweet child—no trouble at all, poor thing."

Mack put a hand on the seamstress's shoulder in calm affirmation, but she shrunk back from his touch. People really did fear him in Treasure Creek. The realization sunk a black hole into the bottom of his stomach. He yearned to be respected, but he had no desire to be feared. Not by good people. "We'll do everything we can to take care of you, Miss Goddard. You have my word, you and Goldie will be safe until we can sort this out."

"Yes," Lana added, "of course. And if you need anything, anything at all, you know we'll help."

"Thank you." Viola smiled as she gave the baby another hug. "Thank you so much." The baby gave out a little coo, reaching up her hand toward the seamstress's beaming face. Viola gazed down at the child. "Everything's going to be just fine now, Goldie, you'll see. I'll take the best care of you." She looked back up at Mack. "And I will. I promise you that."

"I'm sure you will," Mack replied, taking care to make his voice as reassuring as possible. "You get that little one on home and take care. I'll stop by later, once I've had a chance to work out what ought to happen next."

Lana watched the young woman step out into the cool sunshine, tucking the blanket close around the child as she walked. Mack shook his head, shifting his weight back on one hip as, together, they stared after Viola Goddard. "Never saw that coming," he muttered, and she heard genuine surprise in his voice.

"Imagine!" Lana reached for Georgie's hand and hoisted the precious boy up on one hip. "Leaving a child on a doorstep in a place like this. What kind of parent would do such a thing?" *Possibly an Indian parent,* she thought. It was clear this was a native child, despite Viola's doubts. The Indians up here seemed so different—as mysterious and frightening as those she had encountered back in Seattle. Strange dress and language, odd practices no one understood. She always found their music and legends rather dark and disturbing. And to abandon a baby? Lana couldn't think of anything more unsettling. She tried not to be judgmental, but there were those who believed that the Tlingit guides intentionally let Jed and those other miners go up the trail on that dangerous day. "What kind of parent would do such a thing?"

"I suppose we'll find out. We can just pray whoever wrote that note turns up soon." Mack patted the pocket that held the note and gold. "Until then, we'd best keep this quiet."

"It's a baby, Mack. A baby out of nowhere." She looked at him. Even the great and powerful Mack Tanner had limitations. "How on earth are you going to keep this quiet?"

"At the moment, I have no idea. I've got all kinds of plans for all kinds of trouble, but this? This one has me stumped, that's for sure. We'd best take our picnic home today, if you don't mind."

"Of course not." In all the hubbub, she'd forgotten that they planned a picnic lunch for after church services today. It had been Mack's suggestion, his idea of a peace offering, she supposed. It hardly seemed the solution to the problem that just presented itself, but he seemed untroubled. Truly concerned, supportive even, but barely even shocked.

She watched him as he finished shutting up the church for the afternoon, as if the day had been ordinary. She did not even come close to understanding this man. Despite years of acquaintance, they were strangers. She and Mack were so out of sync with each other, so poor at connecting, that their every effort to grow closer seemed to only make things worse.

It didn't help that it seemed to Lana as though her husband was two different men: a darkly righteous judge and a generous protector. How could this man, who'd so quickly condemned Leo to Skaguay, accept a wild abandoned Indian baby story from a woman in town barely two weeks? She'd seen Mack had the capacity to be very kind. Not only in gestures like today's picnic and his muddled attempts at gifts, but emotionally kind. She felt it in the way he treated her the day of their wedding, the times he'd let down his guard playing with Georgie. There had been moments in the last week when she would catch a split second of tremendous warmth in his eyes. Occasionally, he'd place his hand on the small of her back as they walked or stood, and the warmth of it would radiate everywhere. His rough hands would place her shawl over her shoulders with surprising tenderness. She'd felt his gaze more than once and turned to find him staring at her as if her company pleased him greatly. They were becoming true companions. She was no longer alone.

Still, she'd seen firsthand how cold and judgmental he could be. Did his powerful principles ever leave room for mercy? Would he be an overstrict father to Georgie? If she should ever fail to live up to his high standards, what would happen? She didn't know the answer to any of those questions, and it frightened her.

Her tangled thoughts must have shown, for Mack remarked, "You're quiet," as he hoisted Georgie up on his shoulders on the walk home. He was trying to start up a conversation, but he'd chosen the worst possible moment. *Try,* Lana thought to herself. *Try to connect.* She looked around her, willing the scenery to shake the troublesome thoughts from her head. It was a stunning, brilliantly clear day—the kind of Alaskan afternoon that could fuel optimism and hope in the sorriest of souls, just by turning one's face upward to the sun. The mountains jutted proudly to the sky, as if tucking tiny Treasure Creek close to their feet for protection. The water sparkled, and Georgie pointed and shouted to the flocks of birds that swooped and dove over the docks. It really was the perfect day for a picnic—or would have been.

"I suppose I am." She couldn't put her tumble of thoughts into words. Mack wouldn't want to hear them if she could, anyhow.

"Worried about class tomorrow?" he tried again, the words sounding cumbersome and forced.

He couldn't have brought up a more sore subject than school. How on earth should she resume classes after such a fiasco? Then again, did the children even know what Leo had done, since she'd discovered the theft after classes were finished? Of course, in a town as small as Treasure Creek, it seemed foolish to think everyone hadn't known about every detail by now. Mack was far too optimistic if he thought he could keep a secret so dramatic as a Tlingit baby abandoned on a doorstep with a mysterious note and gold. Tomorrow's lessons were supposed to be about weights and measures, but any creativity on the subject loomed as unreachable as the flocks of birds high up over the water. And she certainly couldn't ask for help from Mack—he'd barely supported her efforts as it was.

She was lost in such thoughts until she felt Mack's hand thrust across in front of her, silently blocking her path. "Of all the underhanded..." he growled out, stepping back and sliding Georgie from his shoulders with a "shh" to the boy. She realized with a start that they were about to turn the corner to their house, until Mack pushed her back.

"Hey! You there!" Mack took off at a full sprint, barreling down the last feet of the block to tackle a pair of dirty-looking lads. Rascally boys of no more than twenty, who were, she realized, digging in her yard by the house's foundation! Before she could take six steps, Mack had the pair of them up against the house, pinned by their own shovel.

"What are you up to? As if I didn't know," Mack growled as he forced the wooden handle up against their grimy collarbones.

The larger of them grumbled an unintelligible response. Mack pressed harder, sending the smaller of them into a coughing fit. "Answer me! Were you looking for gold?"

"Isn't everyone?" the larger one wheezed.

"And you figured Sunday morning was a fine time to go prospecting in my yard, seeing as how I'd be leading church services down the block and all." Lana watched Mack's grip on the shovel handle tighten with anger. "Bringing your low-life thieving to my family's front door."

"We heard Nicky Peacock talking in Skaguay 'bout how much gold you had hidden up here. Lots of it, but not in the banks. 'Course we thought it would be here." The smaller one seemed to be under the very dangerous impression that Mack would find this complimentary.

In reality, Lana suspected Mack was clutching the last threads of his temper. Were Georgie not with her, it seemed very likely Mack would be taking their heads off with that shovel, rather than inching it up toward their necks as he was doing at the moment. She pushed Georgie behind her skirts instinctively anyway.

"There is no gold here," Mack snarled. "You'll leave now, go back to whatever crack in Skaguay you crawled out of and never set foot in Treasure Creek again. Am I clear?"

"So we won't look for yours, then. We'll look for the sixteen Russian nuggets instead. We won't bother…" His retort was cut short by the application of the shovel to his neck. He managed a nod, and when Mack released the shovel the pair took off at a run toward the docks.

"Aren't you going to go after them?" Lana thought he might personally deposit the pair into the freezing waters and tell them to swim to Skaguay.

"And leave you and Georgie unprotected? They're not worth it." He tossed the shovel to the ground in disgust. "I don't know which are more dangerous, the clever ones or the stupid ones."

"So, word of the new treasure has reached Skaguay." Lana picked up the food basket she'd dropped and took Georgie's hand. For the first time since that awful morning on the docks, Lana felt a genuine sense of danger. Bravado talk was one thing. Digging up her very house was quite another. "Nicky Peacock?" she ventured in low tones.

"Or others like him. Rumors here flow faster than the tide. I was counting on that, but not on it showing up on my doorstep." His annoyance showed clearly on his face. She knew he'd meant the six nuggets to draw attention *away* from his family, not toward it, but it was clear the plan wasn't working. Today announced that loud and clear. And the boy had said "sixteen," not "six." If word of the nuggets left with Goldie got out, how much worse would the chaos get?

Lana knew Mack thought the bankers little more than crooks, but still her heart sunk when he pulled the baby's gold from his pocket the moment they were inside the house. Even before his coat was off

Mack went to the fireplace mantel. Lana watched him shift the third stone from the left, gasping to herself as it slid aside to reveal a small tin box cemented into the fixture. A hiding place deliberately built into the house. He tucked the gold nuggets and the note from Goldie's mysterious parent inside and slid the stone back. It made Lana wonder just how many more secret hiding places there were. And what all Mack Tanner hid from the world.

Chapter Fourteen

Despite his distraction, Mack stuck to his original idea of a Sunday picnic, even though it had to be in the backyard, rather than out by the beautiful waterfall, as he'd planned. It wasn't working well. The tense small talk he made with Lana felt falsely cheerful, fooling only Georgie as they spread lunch out in a sunny patch by the little garden. To her credit, Lana had leveraged Alaska's long hours of summer daylight, already coaxing enthusiastic sprouts and buds out of the black soil.

"How's the new General Store coming?" she said brightly, as she passed out slices of beef and the thick sourdough bread he'd smelled baking yesterday morning.

"Fine."

No, it wasn't. It was the furthest thing from fine, but he wasn't about to admit that to her now. God had designed wives to be helpmates, he understood that. But this wasn't that kind of marriage.

He couldn't unload his mounting troubles on her still-grieving heart. *How can she be a helpmate to me, Lord? How are we ever going to make this work? We're both stumbling through this, drowning in mistakes.* It would surely be a mistake to admit how things were spinning out of his control lately. Shipments were coming in wrong, there had been six different problems with the counter he and Ed had built yesterday and he was just coming to see how impossible it was going to be to wear General Store manager and mayor hats at the same time. "Busy, but fine." Busy was true. Contrary to his original thoughts, it *had* changed things to be mayor. For the worse. Everyone came to him with every problem now. Every need—logistic and civic—was laid at his feet. Instead of becoming more educated, the stampeders coming through town seemed more and more hoodwinked. Young fools with too many dreams and nowhere near enough equipment. Not to mention nowhere near enough cash—the demands for store credit were practically making him a bank rather than an outfitter. His nightly walks though town used to be times of prayer and praise, giving thanks for Treasure Creek's immense possibilities. Now they were long lamentations, groaning out to God with a list of problems that expanded with every day.

Now this baby business? It was the last kind of complication he needed. And where had Viola Goddard come? Straight to him. Asking for protection he wasn't at all sure how to give.

Lana leaned back against a porch column, the strong sunlight casting gold shimmers into her yellow hair. She licked jam off one finger like a pleased schoolgirl. "Have you thought about how to celebrate the opening?"

"Celebrate it?" Mack leaned back himself. "I figured we'd just open the doors and be done with it."

She huffed. "That's the trouble with you men. No sense of how to celebrate an accomplishment. I suppose you'd find a party a useless frivolity." He watched her back straighten, the way it did when she got an idea. And as he'd discovered, Lana with an idea was one of God's most relentless creatures.

"I would," he said, the uselessness of that objection uncurling an apprehension in his now full stomach.

"And you'd be wrong." She looked at him, eyes narrowed, no sign of the fear that was there a minute ago.

"I would?"

She turned to face him now, pointing at him with her napkin. "People need celebrations. They need to mark their achievements. Towns do, too. Treasure Creek needs a celebration."

"Stores have opened before and no one's thrown a party. Accomplishments speak for themselves, Lana. No one needs to tout them."

"But you're mayor now. It's up to you to give the town what it needs. And it needs a celebration. The opening of Tanner's General Store just happens to provide the opportunity."

So it was Tanner's General Store now, was it? Well, folks called the existing business Tanner's Outfitting Post and this new building was more than that. If forced to name it he probably would have defaulted to Tanner's General Store. Which didn't explain why it bothered him so that Lana already had.

"Tanner's General Store?"

"Well, I assume you were going to name it *something*. What else would you call it but Tanner's General Store?"

Mack didn't want to answer that. He merely grunted, hoping that would signal the end of this absurd conversation.

"I'd do it, you know."

She cocked her head to one side eyes wide in that persuasive manner he'd come to recognize. He could see it coming, knew the result, but found himself powerless against it. "Do what?"

"Plan the party for you. My first official act as… is there a title for the mayor's wife?"

"The *mayor's wife*." He chose not to hide the smile creeping across his face. He knew by the set of his shoulders and the sliding sensation in his heart that there would be a party—a big party—and there wouldn't be a thing he could do to stop it. And oddly enough, there was not very much he wanted to do to stop it. How had the great and stoic Mack Tanner fallen so easily to a woman's persuasion?

"You know—" he was certain victory lit up the corners of her eyes as she said it "—there's another reason to have this party."

"It will require a shopping trip to Skaguay for new dresses?" Mack couldn't remember the last time he'd teased someone. It rather surprised him that he still possessed a sense of humor.

She tossed her napkin at him, and he found himself enjoying the mock scowl on her delicate features. "No. Although I suspect that could be a pleasant consequence. I was talking about a distraction."

Mack highly doubted Treasure Creek's rampant greed could be solved by a party. "Men are not distracted by parties."

"That may be true, but women are very much distracted by parties. And men are very much distracted by women."

Now there was a fact he was coming to know entirely too well lately.

It was almost two o'clock in the morning. The night made only a halfhearted attempt at darkness up here at the height of summer. Lana still couldn't quite get used to the overload of daylight. It robbed her sleep and tangled her sense of time. The house was quiet, the single lamp she'd lit throwing gold and shadows across the room. She'd only now just begun to feel comfortable with the combination of furnishings—things of hers sitting among Mack's things. The new and familiar thrust together jumbled her thoughts as much as the overlong days.

Sleeplessness during the "midnight sun" was a common ailment, but sleep eluded her tonight for a number of reasons. Mack had tried to hide it, but she knew he was highly disturbed at finding that pair of miscreants digging around their house. Goodness, what if he had gone on to Viola's to deal with that baby business and left her and Georgie to walk home on their own? What would have happened then? She'd just begun to allow herself to relax, to ease into the protection her marriage to Mack afforded—to permit the man's strength to loosen the stranglehold of survival that had clutched at her for too long. After this afternoon, that worm of worry had begun to return. What if someone chose to try and get to Mack through Georgie, now that he was his stepfather? She'd heard of kidnappings going on in Skaguay and other towns, but had dismissed them as tall tales.

She couldn't dismiss them now, and she resented the return of her fears and worries. *How, Lord?* Lana surprised herself with the challenging prayer. *How could You let this happen? This is no answer, no stability, no safe haven. If You really do care about how much I need those things, how much Georgie needs them, where is Your provision? I can't see it.*

It felt wrong to whine to God—which was essentially what she was doing—but Lana felt it would be worse to say thankful, pious prayers she didn't mean. According to the commandments Mack preached on this morning, God didn't want His people to steal and covet, to kill each other for gold. Or, she suspected, to leave helpless babies on doorsteps where anything could happen to them. If she was worried about people breaking commandments and hurting her, it seemed only right to take her fears directly to the Almighty, who didn't like such things, either. Mack's prayers were never carefully crafted poetic things, they were heartfelt and intimate conversations with a close and trustworthy God. Admirable as that was, Lana didn't see how the tiny shred of faith she still had could come anywhere near that kind of relationship.

Could it?

She ran her hands across the worn leather cover of Mack's Bible, her finger tracing the remnants of his initials in one corner. This must have been a fine, fancy Bible at one point—the whisper-thin pages had bits of the shiny edges still left on them, and the leather was high quality. It reminded her of the man himself—one could still see the fine and fancy man underneath the ruggedness Alaska demanded. He was such an honorable man. He'd do anything to protect her and Georgie. How on earth could that not be enough?

She hadn't opened a Bible since she'd picked a

psalm to read at Jed's funeral. It felt frightening—dangerous even—to open it now. Still, there was a time when she could take comfort from its verses, even if that did feel like decades ago. With trepidation, Lana placed the volume on her lap and opened it.

"I always start with *Psalms* when I can't sleep," came Mack's voice from the door of his room. How long had he been standing there? She had the illogical panic that he'd heard her rantings to God, even though she was quite sure she'd never said them aloud.

"Did I wake you?" It was a foolish question, but he'd startled the composure right out of her.

"No." He walked into the circle of lamplight, looking mussed and even a bit sad. She hadn't seen this side of him. Even at that dark hour when he came down the mountain with the horrible shrouded bundle on the sled behind him, he'd looked in control. Not a shirt button out of place. Now his shirt was barely buttoned, the tawny muscles of his chest exposed. Mack looked rugged and vulnerable at the same time. As if all kinds of emotional currents ran in the depths of his blue eyes, humming in her chest with every breath. "I've not been able to get a moment's shuteye tonight, either."

His words were the closest thing to an admission of weakness she'd ever heard from him. It uncurled something deep inside, even as she fought against it.

"I like *Psalms,*" Mack said as he walked over to the fireplace and began arranging kindling. The fire shot red-gold into his dark hair, casting a warm glow over his neck and arms. Even tired and mussed, the man exuded strength. "I like that David argued with God. Or yelled, or complained, or demanded. Straight shooter, that David. Always let God know where he stood. I'd like to think God returned the favor."

Mack always talked about God in the most surprising ways. Ways that seemed impossible for ordinary folk. Combined with the intensity of his character, it was easy to believe Mack had some kind of Almighty connection mere mortals couldn't achieve. "What's that got to do with why I can't sleep?" Lana said. She'd been careful not to say anything about her growing fears all evening. He was so protection-minded, she was afraid if she showed even the smallest fear he'd lock her in the house under guard.

"Well," Mack blew the flames higher and added another log, "I am rarely up nights thinking how fine everything is. Most folks sleep well when they're happy, even if it is light at ten o'clock." He craned his neck over his shoulder and managed the sort of smile women would swoon over. A dark but dashing look—the heartbreaker of years past and fortunes won.

"It's the light," she lied, returning the book to its

place on the side table. "I don't know that I'll ever get used to it."

"Actually, it hasn't bothered me nearly as much lately." He eased himself into the chair, but not before he buttoned his shirt properly and took the Bible from where she'd returned it. "I have these things called curtains now. Handy contraptions to keep the light out."

Lana rolled her eyes, suppressing a smile. "Imagine that."

"I'm eating better, too."

He'd always been incapable of a direct compliment. Still, he was trying, she had to give him that much. "Are you now?"

"'Course, my house is always in a ruckus and I've tripped over blocks twice this week. That's new, too."

She narrowed her eyes at him. "How very difficult for you." She knew very well how well Georgie could try a soul. Did he stop to think how hard it was on Georgie? Death and strife and uprooting to a new home?

"It's a challenge."

It was as if he'd buttoned up the vulnerability as easily as he'd buttoned up the shirt. The unshakable, no room for doubt persona was back full force. It left Lana wondering if she'd really seen his guard down seconds ago or just imagined it. "All parenting is," she replied, "I suspect you gave your mama quite the run for her money."

A crack reappeared in the facade and his face darkened. "I wouldn't know. I didn't know her at all. I was only two when she died."

"I hadn't realized you lost her so young. I'm sorry." He'd lost his mother at the same age Georgie lost his father. Perhaps that was why he was so adamant Georgie have her full attention.

"My brothers told me stories of her. They didn't remember much, but they knew her some. And my father would talk about her all the time, so in a sense she was still real to me. I knew her favorite songs, her favorite colors and foods, her favorite psalm, lots of things."

His eyes seemed to gaze back into memory, and Lana realized that all those people he'd just spoken of—father and brothers—were all gone, too. The question slipped out of her mouth before she'd even realized it. "What was her favorite psalm?"

Mack flipped the book open. "The Twenty-third—like lots of folks."

She didn't want him to read it. She was somehow afraid of what the familiar words would do to her, especially in his voice, especially from a man who had lost as much if not more than she had.

"The Lord is my shepherd," he began, and Lana felt her throat tighten. *"I shall not want."*

She'd heard those words dozens of times, but despite Mack's soft voice, the words hit her like sledgehammers. Green pastures? Spreading a table? Words of abundance and security, things she craved so much, the ache in her chest seem to expand too far too fast.

"Yea, though I walk through the valley of the shadow of death, I will fear no evil, for Thou art with me."

She had walked every single step of the valley of the shadow of death. Felt every jagged inch of the path through that horrible place, but she feared evil. The kind of trust these words portrayed was far beyond her wounded heart's capacity. Lana felt a double edge cut through her: a desperate yearning for the faith he described, and a heavy sense of her complete inability to achieve it.

Mack seemed to sense her turmoil, for he fell silent when he finished the psalm. Lana felt fragile, as if one wrong word from him would shatter her— and he was so good at saying or doing just the wrong thing. She found herself holding her breath, fighting the urge to run from the room, and yet somehow rooted to her chair.

"He is with us," he said after a long pause.

Lana felt twelve emotions at once. For once, Mack Tanner had said the exact right thing.

Chapter Fifteen

He'd read the Bible to her. Actually, he hadn't even read it, for he knew the words of the beloved psalm by heart. Mack's father had said that it was possible to watch the words of scripture pierce a heart, that there were times the power of God's word showed so clearly on someone's face, it was like watching a wound. Or a healing.

He'd just seen it. On the face of his wife.

He stared at her bedroom door long after Lana left the room. She'd undone him, pure and simple. The jolt of protective panic he'd felt when they'd discovered that pair digging in the yard was bad enough. He was so overcome with fury that someone might endanger his family—yes, he'd come to think of it as *his* family now—that he'd been violent. He'd wondered, in his darker moments, if Georgie's presence behind him had been the only thing keeping him from doing serious harm to those boys. He surely wanted to wring their necks for their greedy stupidity. And perhaps his own fool-ishness—his plan of the diversionary six nuggets wasn't working.

Everything was going wrong. The store was way behind schedule, the last city council meeting had not only been a fiasco, it had resulted in his mayor-ship, there was this new twist of Viola Goddard's mystery baby and he was supposed to have the solu-tions for all of these! All of Treasure Creek seemed to be pressing down on him, clawing away at his composure, keeping him up nights as surely as the midnight sun.

While sun and town may have kept him up tonight, what was going to rob the rest of tonight's sleep was the current pounding in his chest. Mack hadn't mentioned his mother in years. Hadn't opened up that black box of memory for anyone since his father had passed. How was it that Lana could pry it open without the slightest effort? How was it he would have stayed up all night telling her things he hadn't spoken of to anyone else? She was so much smarter than he'd ever given her credit for, fooled as he was by her preoccupation with ruffles and baubles. There was much more to her than he ever would have guessed.

He liked that.

She tugged words, thoughts and feelings out of him in ways he didn't like to admit. Mack was com-fortable with the obligation of his marriage, had even hoped for friendship, but he was more than a little unraveled at the thing currently uncurling in his chest. It felt dangerously close to attraction. And Georgie…well, Georgie seemed entirely too able to pull a confounding tenderness from him. The pair of them, Lana and Georgie, panicked him, made him do foolish things. What kind of steady-hearted man could suggest a picnic and go after thugs with a shovel in the same Sunday? What kind of man could read his mother's favorite Bible verse to a woman in one second, and be broadsided by the urge to hold her in the next? She looked so frail in that moment, so undone by God's word, that all these inexplicable emotions had come roaring to life in him.

And what had he done? He'd said the wrong thing. "He is with us." Could he, preacher's son that he was, come up with nothing more eloquent than that? Of course God was with them—God was with them every moment of every day. Lana didn't need platitudes, she needed clear comfort, a better promise of protection to calm her spirit. And what had he given her? Four measly words. Which obviously hadn't helped, for she'd teared up and quit the room about as fast as she could, managing a stumbling good-night with hardly a look back. *I can't sort her out, Lord,* he said with his hand on the Bible, as if trying to recover the sensation of her hand on the worn leather cover. *I can't provide for her if I don't know how.*

The celebration idea seemed to spark something in her. As foolish as he found such a party, she seemed to think it grand. And perhaps, as diversions went, it had merit. People seemed to need Treasure Creek to have all the trappings of a real town— mayor, town council meetings. Why not a summer festival of some sort? Treasure Creek ought to celebrate its growth, ought to give corporate thanks for the blessings God had granted.

Her party idea actually made sense.

And made her happy. While he wouldn't currently admit it to another living soul, making Lana Tanner happy was a very satisfying prospect indeed.

School went so smoothly the next morning that Lana walked over to the new schoolhouse right after classes.

Lana decided to launch the first step in her grand scheme while her confidence was high. Mack hadn't actually said he agreed to the idea, but if she could get the Tuckers behind it, he'd have no choice but to see the merit in her plan.

She was surprised and sad at how much calmer the classroom had become with Leo gone. Had be been more disruptive than she realized? She couldn't ignore the sense of relief she felt from the students, unfortunate as it was. Still, some part of her yearned for the satisfaction of helping Leo reach his potential. Helping all of them reach their potential. They had so much. The whole town was capable of so much.

"A what?" Frankie Tucker balked, after Lana laid

out her plans for the "Midsummer Festival." Taking off her hat and scratching her head, Frankie looked as if she'd just been asked to wrestle a bear.

"A party. A townwide party when the General Store opens." Lana looked her straight in the eye, as if it was the most natural idea in all the world, ignoring Frankie's baffled expression.

Lucy Tucker waved the hammer she'd been using to finish a windowsill on the new school. "For everyone? Like a church social or somethin'?"

"Very nearly. It'd be for Mack's store, but that's more of an excuse. Everyone loves a chance to get gussied up, no matter what the cause. We could simply call it a Midsummer Festival. Parties bring folks together, don't you think?" Lana looked at Frankie, who barely changed into clean pants for Sunday services, and wondered if the boisterous woman even owned a party dress. If Viola had a new mouth to feed, she might welcome the new business a prospective party would bring. Every hour, some new reason for the festival seemed to be coming to her. Grand plans were one of Lana's favorite pastimes, her daddy used to always say. Of course, he'd be a bit stumped by what passed for "a grand time" up here, but that couldn't be helped.

Margie Tucker leaned her weight on the plank she was holding. "I don't know if you noticed, but we're not much for shindigs up here. You're as likely to get a row as you are to get a celebration." Margie knew of what she spoke—she'd broken up nearly as many dock fights as Mack had.

"But we didn't get a wedding when you got hitched," Lucy added, with a funny look that made Lana think Lucy blamed her for that oversight, "so I suppose we're due. But we aren't the kind to help you with that sort of thing. I don't know why you're asking us, really." Lucy looked down at Georgie, who was amusing himself with the long yellow curls of log shavings at her feet. "What do you think, Georgie? You like parties?"

"Because," Lana said sweetly, not falling for the diversion, "if *you're* for it, no one would dare disagree." It was true. Whether it was for the sheer novelty of the Tuckers in party dress, or fear of defying the tough-as-nails trio, Lana didn't care. Both worked.

She watched as the three sisters exchanged glances among themselves. "Caleb Johnson was saying the other day, how he missed all the county fairs he had in summers back home. I suppose I could fancy a party. I mean, it couldn't hurt none to have one," Lucy offered, clearly waiting for Frankie's take as eldest sister.

"You're not gonna make us get gussied up or anything, are you?" Margie's suspicious tone almost made Lana laugh.

"That'd be up to you, of course. We don't have everything worked out just yet," Lana conceded. "I just thought you'd like to be the first to know."

Now, this was the way to the Tuckers' collective hearts. The Tucker sisters liked to be at the center of everything—even if it was a fight—and being first in on a big scoop like this pleased them immensely. Not that they were gossips. They were women of incredible faith and integrity, actually. They never lied; just the opposite, a Tucker would tell you the straight truth, whether or not you wanted to hear it.

"You're asking us if we approve?" Frankie crossed her arms over her barrel of a chest, puffing a lock of unruly dark hair off her forehead.

Lana folded her hands, ready to wait if necessary. "People care what you think." Paradoxical or not, it was true. Despite the fact that the Tuckers gave little thought to what others thought of them, everyone in Treasure Creek held their opinion in high regard. Those opinions did sometimes come backed up with an occasional fist, so that may have been part of the reason.

"Not that it's *my* idea of a good time," Lucy declared from over yet another nail, "but I suspect someone like Caleb would think a festival is a good step for the town…if you can keep it from getting out of hand."

That was Lucy, always qualifying every idea with a hint of doubt. For all her boldness, she could be as recalcitrant as a mule. Her drab habit of dressing in blacks and grays only strengthened the image for Lana. "Mack will take care of that," she replied, knowing that it was the accepted answer for just about any trouble in Treasure Creek.

And that was the trouble with Treasure Creek. They looked to Mack for everything, and it had only doubled since his "election" as Mayor. She had an idea for that, too, but it would have to be broached very carefully.

"Well, then." Frankie's voice took on a tone of declaration. "I can't say I'm against it."

While not a rousing endorsement, it was all Lana needed. She smiled broadly. "Time to get going, Georgie." Georgie picked up two of the long, loopy wooden shavings, bouncing them like springs with a giggle, and stood up to go. Still, Georgie was smart enough to remember who the Tucker sisters were and what they usually carried. He looked up at Lucy with wide, brown eyes.

Lucy beamed. "Well now, little fella, all you have to do is ask."

Georgie carefully transferred both shavings to one hand and held out the other chubby palm. "Peez?"

Lucy dug into the upper pocket of her overalls to produce a hanky of questionable cleanliness, unwrapping a "cookie." Lana could never cease to amaze herself with the unappetizing colors of the Tuckers' "baking." The disc looked more like hardware than baked goods. "There's a good young man," Lucy said as she blew something off the top of the cookie and handed it to Georgie. *The boy hasn't gotten sick yet.* Lana reminded herself that she'd found her precious son out in the garden yesterday, gnawing on a dirty root. Still, she hoped he'd keep all his teeth. The sharp snap his bite of cookie made set her own teeth to aching as she helped Georgie wave goodbye with the handful of shavings. Step One had been accomplished.

She tried not to feel surprised when she found herself in cautious prayer that Step Two would meet with equal success.

The certainty of it had settled upon him while fitting the last of the shelving in the General Store. Mack had known it for weeks, months even, but as he and Ed struggled to get the final planks onto their brackets, it pressed on Mack so clearly he couldn't deny it any longer: He needed help. Treasure Creek needed a preacher and a sheriff far more than it had ever needed a mayor, and it was high time to do something about it.

Every Bible passage he read over the past month seemed to be about partnerships, about Apostles going out in pairs, Moses and Aaron, Timothy and Paul. His own home, running more smoothly than ever despite Georgie's constant motion, spoke just as loudly about the virtues of shared labor. Mack needed partners.

When they took a moment to sit and have a drink of water after the shelf was wedged into place and secured, Mack forged ahead. He looked Ed straight in the eye and made his case. "Ed, you should be sheriff." Mack had given the matter quite a bit of thought, and while he could name a few folks who'd readily volunteer, none of them would come near doing the job Ed would.

Ed seemed a bit shocked to hear it. Surprise flickered across his face, followed by an unsettling chuckle. "Should I now? Didn't know Treasure Creek had the position open, to tell the truth."

Mack remembered the scene at the most recent town meeting and narrowed his eyes at Ed. "It followed fast on the heels of mayor, if you must know. Sort of a one-two punch."

Ed made a "you got me," face, followed by a long, drawn out pause of thought. "I'm not the man," he said, pulling one broad hand over his neatly trimmed beard.

"'Course you are." It was weak, as arguments went, but Mack hadn't at all anticipated Ed's refusal. A bit of reluctance maybe, or just surprise, but Mack never expected his offer to be turned down. Ed was practically doing the job now, it was in his very nature.

"Nope. I don't think so. Breaking up the occasional fight, that's one thing. But *being* the law? Having to answer to folks and fill out papers and such? I'd only let you down."

Mack was genuinely stumped. Too much about Treasure Creek was stumping him lately. "I'd want you to be sheriff, Ed. Anybody would."

"I'd want to sink my shovel in my backyard and hit a lode of gold, but that don't mean I'd be digging in the right place."

Ed gave out a sigh that hinted there was a long, untold story behind his refusal, reminding Mack he didn't actually know that much about Ed. He was a big bear of a man, burly to be sure, but upright and faithful, too. Maybe he had a questionable past, but didn't half of Alaska? Ed was as reliable as they came. Mack was sure he was the man for the job. "You should be sheriff," he repeated.

Ed's only response was to give Mack a conversation ending stare. Dark and declarative. "No, I shouldn't," he said quietly as he stood up and brushed the sawdust off his trousers. "I'm going to find some lunch." It was not an invitation.

"I guess I'll just shave the last of these cabinet doors." Mack stood there, rubbing his chin with the back of one hand, and watched his friend fill the doorway with his enormous shoulders and then disappear.

That went dandy, he thought sourly. If God was asking him to find partners, the least He could do was prod them to say "yes" when asked.

Chapter Sixteen

Lana's skirts swept through the doorway a second later, and she was staring in the direction Ed had gone. Mack's annoyance must have been all over his face, for she was barely in the room before she said, "What's going on with the two of you?"

Mack really didn't want to get into this with her. She had that sunny look on her face, the one that meant she was ankle-deep in one of those ideas of hers, and it always meant trouble. "We had a disagreement," he said, hoping it would end the conversation as effectively as Ed's glare, but knowing it wouldn't.

Georgie came from behind her, bouncing a pair of long wood shavings with a ridiculous grin on his face. She came over to stand in front of him, arms crossed over her chest. "You two? Over what?"

There was no help for it. She'd get it out of him sooner or later. "I told him he should be sheriff and he said no."

Lana's eyebrows shot up. "Sheriff?"

"It's high time we got one, don't you think?"

She undid the strings of her bonnet and took it off. "As a matter of fact, I do. And Ed's a smart choice. But he didn't want to be sheriff when you asked him?"

Mack stuffed his hands into his pockets. "I told him he should be sheriff and he said 'no, I shouldn't.' Just like that."

Lana eyed him. He really didn't like it when Lana eyed him that way. "Just like that?"

"Like what?"

"You told him he ought to be sheriff." She placed her bonnet down carefully on the new store counter. "Is that how you put it?"

"He ought to be sheriff. I didn't think much about *how I put it*."

Lana folded her hands in front of her. "Well, I can see that."

"Just what is that supposed to mean?"

"Mack, people don't like to be told things like that. They like to be asked. Maybe you needed to ask Ed if he would *consider* being sheriff. Tell him why he'd be your first choice for the job."

Ed? Practical, forthright Ed? "I suppose I ought to have written out an invitation and had him over for dinner to discuss the advantages?"

He was being sarcastic but she rose straight to his bait. "As a matter of fact, it wouldn't have hurt."

"I need a sheriff, not a diplomat. He knows he's

the man for the job. He's practically doing it now. I don't see the problem."

Lana's hands went to her hips. "No, you don't, do you? Do you know, Mack Tanner, that you never once *asked* me to marry you? No, you *told* me I *ought* to marry you. Insistently."

Mack's hands flew up in the air. "Well, it worked, didn't it?"

Sparks flew from her eyes. "Only barely."

Huffing, Mack stomped to the other side of the room and began pulling the top off a crate of newly delivered hardware.

She followed him. "You cannot simply inform the world of your plans. Well, I suppose if you want to manage the entire world on your own, be running from dawn until midnight the way you are, and not get help from all the good people ready to help you…"

"I don't see anyone lining up to help me," he growled.

"No, because you won't look. For a man who wants to run a town, you've got an awful lot to learn about people." She put out her tiny little hand and slapped down the lid he was lifting. Glory but she was a feisty, infuriating thing. "You can't just go ordering them around." She was using that too-clear teacher voice of hers, and it rankled him.

"I don't."

"You do."

"He's a grown man, Lana, not some child I have to coddle."

"Making a civilized request of a grown man is not coddling him."

"No one asked me if I want to be mayor, now, did they? Look at Ed. He was in on that from the first. No one said one word about 'whether or not I'd *consider* taking the job.'"

Lana fiddled with the lace at her cuff. "That was different."

"No, it isn't."

"We all knew you'd say yes."

"No one…" Mack stopped in his tracks. "What do you mean, 'we'? Did you know about that?" He furrowed his eyebrows at her. "Were you in on that?" She was. He could tell by the way she licked her lips and hesitated. Was there no end the trouble this woman would cause him?

"As a matter of fact, I was consulted."

He hated it when she got that prim and proper tone to her voice. "How?" He drew the word out, long and menacing.

"Ed asked me if I thought you'd agree."

Mack sat back on his heels and rued the day she'd consented to anything. "And…"

"And I told him I was certain you'd say yes, and that it would be good for you and the town to boot."

Good for him. He hadn't had a moment's peace or privacy in weeks and this was *good for him*. "I'm not going to strong-arm Ed into doing something he doesn't want to do. That's good for no one."

Lana began to wander around the store, poking into this and that. Was she going to rearrange his store the way she'd rearranged the house? She probably thought that would be good for him, too. He watched her eye the set of shelves he'd just put up and decided helpmates were highly overrated. "Ed should be sheriff," she said, running her hand along the side of the shelf in a way that made him worry she was measuring for ruffled fringe. "You're right about that."

Mack sat down on the barrel of assorted hardware that had arrived yesterday. Two weeks late and with only half the items he'd ordered. "That's exactly what I said to him, you know."

"We'll just have to ask him in a way that helps him to realize just how perfect he is for the job."

There was that "we" again. "Oh, surely." Normally, he wasn't much for sarcasm, but she seemed to bring out his more exasperated traits.

She brushed the sawdust from her hands and picked up her bonnet. "Well, I'd better get over to the market and see what I can find if we're going to have Ed over for dinner tomorrow night."

Now who was telling and not asking? "I wasn't aware we'd invited Ed over to dinner tomorrow night." He suddenly felt like Georgie trying to argue his way out of a bath—outranked.

"I'll ask him right now." She lifted her delicate

pale chin with an aristocratic air as she tied the bonnet underneath. "Oh, and the Tucker sisters have weighed in their full support for the Midsummer Festival. They're delighted at the idea."

He highly doubted that. If they'd only agreed not to put up a stink about it, Mack was sure the entire state of Alaska would pull a collective gasp of surprise.

Lana put on her gloves and held out a hand for Georgie. "Viola should have a host of new dress business before the celebration. If the Tuckers are getting new dresses for the occasion, I gather half the town will follow suit. That's good business for everybody, Mr. Mayor. Come, Georgie. We're going to make Mr. Parker a pie."

Tuckers in dresses? Festivals? Pie? Mack stood in shock, staring long after the mesmerizing swish of his wife's skirts. *Hang me,* he thought as he shook his head, *I've just been outmaneuvered. And I think I enjoyed it.*

Lana preferred not to venture too close to the docks these days, but today was the day what little produce made it up to Treasure Creek arrived by boat. If she waited for any of it to find its way up to the little fruit and vegetable stand in town, the best blueberries would be gone. And if there was one thing that grew sweet and splendid in Alaska, it was berries. "Mr. Parker would like a blueberry pie, don't you think, Georgie?"

"Pie!" Georgie endorsed with a grin.

Lana was just saying goodbye to little Hank Duke's parents after complimenting the couple on their son's advancements in reading, when a well-dressed man sauntered up. She hadn't noticed him standing there, listening to her praises of Hank. He flashed a broad smile. "So you are the illustrious new Mrs. Tanner? How pleased I am to meet you. I was an associate of your late husband's. My condolences on your loss, and that of poor…George, isn't it?" he said, tipping his bowler. "How do you like your new papa, George? He's an old friend of mine, Mack is."

There was something in his tone that Lana did not care for at all. "Yes, I am Mrs. Tanner. Mack's just up seeing to the new store. You can find him there. I just left him."

"I've no need to bother Mack. I'm quite sure you can help me. You see, it's come to my attention that a child has arrived in town. A very particular child, kin of mine, to be exact."

So much for keeping word of the gold and baby quiet, Lana thought. Still, the man looked as if he could spare two gold nuggets easily, although he didn't show the concern she thought a relative should have regarding a child left alone in the world. "Kin of yours?" Lana kept a tight grip Georgie's hand. "Mack will be delighted to know the child is kin of an associate. We've been hoping you'd show soon, Mr.…."

"Brown."

Lana had the niggling suspicion that Brown was not this man's real name. Berries or no berries, this man was going straight to Mack as soon as she could lead him. "I'll take you to Mack right now. I know he'll be eager to speak with you. We've all been so concerned."

Mr. "Brown" leaned closer. He smelled little bit of brandy and cigars and quite a lot like a rat. "As have I, Mrs. Tanner, as have I. So I'm sure that, as a parent yourself, you understand my sense of urgency. I'd feel so much better if I could just go straight to seeing the poor little one. Ease my mind over his safety."

His safety? Now Lana knew she smelled a rat. She applied her most charming smile. "Oh, but Mack has taken the matter under his own personal supervision. I'd never dream of overstepping him on this. Surely you'd want us to watch over the little boy with the utmost of care? We couldn't hand him off to any impostor who came calling now, could we?"

"It seems the reputation of Treasure Creek's outstanding character is indeed well earned." He swept his hand grandly around the docks. Lana noticed his fine suit coat wasn't exactly in his size. Mr. Brown had either lost a considerable amount of weight recently, or he ought to fire his tailor.

As she caught site of Ed Parker turning the corner, Lana knew what to do. "Why, Ed Parker, you're just the fellow we need," she said loudly, walking straight up to Ed and clasping his hand. "Ed, dear, this here is Mr. Brown. A close associate of Jed's *and* an old friend of Mack's. Surely you remember him? And guess what? He's come to collect his abandoned baby *boy*." She kept her back to the schemer behind her, raising her eyebrows repeatedly at Ed and saying a quick silent prayer that Parker would catch her ruse and play along. "Isn't it amazing that a friend of Mack's is kin to that poor little boy with all that gold? It's an absolute blessing that he's found us so quickly. He doesn't want to bother Mack or be any trouble. He just wants us to take him straight to that precious baby boy."

Mr. Brown came up behind Lana. "I've been most worried about him. Sad, sad story. I told my nephew Treasure Creek would be a place for him to settle. Shame he never made it. I still don't know how the boy found his way here, but thank the good Lord he did. I'd like to see him right away."

Lana was relieved when Ed patted her hand and began leading Mr. Brown in a direction away from Viola Goddard's house. "Oh, God's been watching over him indeed. He's in fine shape, considering all he's been through."

"All of his belongings arrive safe and sound?"

Lana set her teeth. She could just imagine which of Goldie's "belongings" held Mr. Brown's attention. They were now walking in the direction of Mac-Dougal's blacksmith shop, which not only doubled as the post office, but tripled as the town jail when necessary. Based on the growl that crept into Ed Parker's voice as they continued to talk about Mr. Brown's "poor kin," the man would be lucky if he made it in there without a bruise…or six.

As the four of them—Ed, "Mr. Brown," Lana and Georgie—reached the blacksmith's, Parker looked Lana square in the eye. "Mrs. Tanner," he said as his beefy hand came down fast and hard on Brown's arm, "It's best young Georgie leaves now."

His voice was so menacing, his fury over the sheer arrogance of Brown's extensive lies so barely contained, that Lana didn't put up a word of argument. She scooped Georgie up and set off at a quick pace toward the General Store, even as Brown's cries of alarm rose up behind her. "We're going to let strong Mr. Parker deal with that bad man," she said in reassuring tones, as Georgie kept peering at the commotion behind her.

Mack made her tell the story for the fourth time as they sat on the cabin's front porch that evening. He shook his head, just as he had with each telling, only now he was pacing back and forth across the planks. Rather than ease his concerns, her repetitions made things worse.

"I'm fine," she assured when he made an exasperated sound in the back of his throat. For the third time today.

He stopped pacing and looked at her as if she'd

spoken nonsense. "You could have been killed. Or harmed. Trying to match wits with the likes of him—you were out of your mind!"

"I succeeded. You seem to forget that." Yes, of course she knew she took some risks, but what was she to do? Simply lead the man to a defenseless child? She was rather proud of her actions, but Mack obviously didn't share her opinion.

He turned and grabbed her by the shoulders. "Don't you ever do anything like that again. Ever." It was the closest thing to an actual panic she'd ever seen in Mack. More alarming still, a deep care lit fire to his eyes. This was not the dominant protector she'd known before, but something more. The fright in his eyes and the strength of his grip told of deep concern. Genuine care. As if she and Georgie had come to really mean something to him. It stunned her, locking her to her spot on the planks more surely than his grip on her shoulders. "I couldn't bear it if…"

And then, as if he'd just now realized he was holding her, he froze. She could see him choose a more distant expression, see the mask fall over his face. He tried to release his hands casually, but to no avail. They both knew he had touched her more in those seconds than any other time in their marriage. Even with his hands gone, warmth and pressure lingered far too long. They turned from each other, staring falsely out over the porch rail in a cumbersome silence.

"Be more careful." The familiar command returned to his voice.

She chose not to argue, but instead rested against the porch rail and tried to wade through the flood of her thoughts.

"It's getting out of hand." She wasn't sure he said it to her or to himself. After another long pause he added, "I need Ed."

"Yes," she replied, daring a sideways glance at him. It was as if the storm of tension had passed over them, leaving a tangled calm in its place. "You do."

Mack leaned back against the porch pillar, crossing his arms over his chest. "So tell me again how we go about asking him."

Chapter Seventeen

"Sixty nuggets?" Mack couldn't believe his ears when Duncan MacDougal told him the latest treasure rumor just after Mack ordered shelving brackets. The jack-of-many-trades blacksmith had been known to embellish a tale or two, but this felt beyond even Klondike rumor mill standards.

"Yep, that's the word. It's been good for business, actually. More folks coming straight here to look around while they get outfitted, rather than waiting in Skaguay."

Mack's very clever plan was beginning to seem like a harebrained scheme instead. One that was quickly exploding beyond his control, and with the exact opposite results he was seeking. Mack was used to success. This was feeling far too much like failure for his liking.

"I heard one fella come in here saying there weren't sixty, but sixteen, and each of them was the size of a man's fist. He came looking for the best way to break them into smaller pieces so he could hide them better."

Gold nuggets the size of a man's fist? Not only was that improbable, the weight alone would make it almost impossible to carry. Mack had to smile. "So sure he'd find them, he was already making security plans?"

Duncan heaved his bellows and the fire pit next to him blazed bright orange. "So, Mack, are they really out there?"

It was a game they played, always trying to outwit the other. They were actually on the same side. Mack never deliberately hid things from Duncan out of suspicion; it was always just so much fun to watch the man figure things out. And while Duncan's trades put him in a position to hear anything that was circulating around town, Mack knew he'd never hold back vital information. No, that sooty, redheaded brute simply took pleasure in teasing Mack with all the incendiary gossip he knew. Being forthright with each other would just take all the fun out of it. "What makes you think I know?"

Duncan flexed his big hand in the thick leather glove he always wore and pulled a glowing piece of metal from the pit. "The fact that you do."

Mack chose a diversionary tactic. "I need something other than those brackets. A bit of an unusual order, and one you need to keep it to yourself. Can I trust you?"

That got Duncan's attention. Mid-swing, he

stopped working and returned the strip of iron back to its place within the embers. "What kind of a question is that?"

Of course, Mack knew he could trust Duncan implicitly, but this was too much of an opportunity to squander. "I'll need discretion here. No one can know you're working on this. I'm not even sure you can do it, actually."

Duncan took that personally, his red eyebrows knitting together. "And what is it you need now?"

Pulling a drawing from his coat pocket, Mack laid the illustration of a tin sheriff's star on the counter between them. "I need it by four o'clock today."

Duncan pulled off his gloves and picked up the paper, his eyes darting from Mack to the star. "You're mad. I can't do this on such short notice." After a moment, he raised one eyebrow and whispered, "Who?"

Mack knew he had him. "Can you do it?"

"You haven't got the time to take this to anyone else. I'd skin you if you did, besides. So, who is gonna be the new sheriff?"

"Can't say at the moment." It had been Lana's idea to have the star ready when they had Ed over to dinner. He had to say, it was a brilliant piece of persuasion. And he wouldn't be surprised if Duncan dropped everything and had the star ready within the hour, just to weasel out of Mack the identity of the chest to which it would be pinned. "So," Mack said conversationally, "have you got a kilt to wear to the Midsummer Festival, or will you dress civilized like the rest of us?"

Duncan grunted, both at the blatant diversion and the implied "insult." In a fit of familial pride one night, the Scotsman had vowed—or was it *threatened?*—to break out the MacDougal plaid for Christmas Eve services, when the town reached its first Christmas later this year. Considering what the average temperature would be in Treasure Creek in December, Mack thought it more a declaration of bravery than anything else. Given that the festival would prove less of a test of the man's endurance, Mack suspected the revered MacDougal plaid might indeed make an early appearance.

"So there really is to be a party?"

"Lana's up to her elbows in plans already. So, MacDougal, will it be a kilt or Sunday best?"

He knew Duncan would never dream of satisfying him with an answer. But Mack already had what he needed—the conversation shifted off his association with the gold nuggets—so it mattered little. "Can't say at the moment." Duncan threw Mack's own words back at him as he narrowed one eye, aimed, and took a mighty whack at the strip of iron. "But you'll be the last to know."

"I'd expect nothing less."

Another whack. "Letter came for you yesterday." He said it like an afterthought, but Mack knew he'd withheld it until the last moment. "Something official-like from Skaguay."

Leo. The brief letter stated that Leo had been released two days ago after what the sheriff called a "troublesome" stint in jail. He hadn't come home. All Mack could surmise was that the incarceration hadn't served as the deterrent he'd hoped. It didn't mean all was lost. He'd send letters this afternoon to connections in Skaguay, and do what he could to find Leo before he made new friends he didn't need.

Ed's dinner had turned out perfectly. While Mack had scoffed at the culinary campaign earlier, his smile had broadened as the night went on. Ed was clearly softening to the idea, even though it hadn't been directly spoken of at all. They'd talked in terms of the town's future, of the importance of its character, about how Treasure Creek would be a community where the law mattered.

Lana knew that much of Mack's high-minded speech was for Ed's benefit, but it wasn't for show. Conviction burned in his eyes as he talked of his vision for the town. He deeply believed in the need for a place like Treasure Creek. Not just because honesty and integrity were rare and lofty ideals in this part of the world, but because he'd lived the consequences of lies and deception. Hadn't they both? Yes, Jed's greed had given his faults free rein up here, but he'd been happily egged on by far too many men glad to indulge his weaknesses. Alaska was a place where wisdom was overpowered by cunning, and far too many people paid for it with their lives. Listening to Mack talk, she could feel the spark of his vision catch in her own spirit. To feel the strength of his character undergird her own. She respected him. Watching his eyes tonight, listening to him pour out his heart, her respect was changing into a deeper, surprising care. She was coming to care for Mack Tanner—for the man he was, the father he could be and the world he wanted to make for their family.

After pie—pie which had come out perfectly, sweet and delectable from the last crate of blueberries from this week's shipment of produce—Mack caught her eyes with a hint of a smile as he stood and turned toward the sideboard. "Edward Parker," Lana said, just as they'd planned it earlier, "I am so grateful for what you did yesterday to save poor Goldie. You are a man of honor and strength, and I know anyone who cares about that poor baby girl knows you saved her life. And Viola's, too, perhaps."

"I don't think it was all that," Ed said, flushing from her wordy compliment.

"It was. Too many folks know her story as it is. I'm glad you were there to defend her." Mack took the pouch that had been sitting on the sideboard and placed it solemnly in front of Ed. "Goldie just proves a point. I need your help. Treasure Creek could sure use your help. I want...I *hope*," he corrected himself with a flicker of a look toward Lana, who'd suggested such wording, "you'll consider how much you could do for Treasure Creek by becoming sheriff."

Mack nodded at Ed, who opened the pouch and pulled out a shiny silver star with the words "Treasure Creek Sheriff" etched into it. If she hadn't seen it with her own eyes, she'd have never believed Duncan MacDougal capable of such finely detailed work. It was as if the world lined up to make this request simply perfect.

"I think God sent you here for just this reason," Lana added, surprised that the thought of God's world lining up in perfection slipped so naturally into her head, "and I hope you'll give Mack's request serious consideration. I do believe you're the man for the job. And I know Mack does, too. I want Georgie to grow up in a safe place."

Georgie, who was beginning to nod off from his own big meal, roused at the sound of his name and babbled a few incoherent but enthusiastic comments, ending with "star!" as he pointed to the badge Ed held. Mack had taught him the word earlier today as the whole family inspected Duncan's handiwork.

Ed smiled—he'd always had a soft heart where Georgie was concerned. Lana suspected the big man's resistance was all but dissolved. A great, big heart beat inside that enormous, powerful man. He

would be the embodiment of justice and mercy…
if he took the job.

"Please," Lana said, truly meaning it.

"I need your help." The gruffness in Mack's voice
told Lana what it cost her husband to make that
admission. She was, at that moment, immensely
proud of him.

"I don't see how…" Ed said with a huge sigh,
and Lana heard Mack suck in a breath to try one
more round of convincing, "…I can say no." Ed
finished with something very near a twinkle in his
eye. "Three Tanners against one Parker is hardly
fair odds. Best I give in now and save us all a heap
of fuss." With a fumbling of his thick fingers, he
fixed the silver star to the leather vest he wore.
Mack shook his hand, Lana rewarded the new sheriff with a second slice of pie, and Georgie barked
"star!" over and over while pointing to Ed's swelled
chest.

Mack couldn't stop himself from smiling the rest
of the night. He allowed himself, just for the briefest
of moments, to bask in the reassurance of having
a partner again. Someone to watch his back. He'd
not allowed himself that luxury since Jed's death,
and his spirit ached more at the absence than he
was ready to admit. Ed probably had no idea how
deeply his remark about "three Tanners" had hit—it
had been too long since anyone could use the name
Tanner in plural. His father and brothers were gone,

but now he had a *family*. He hadn't told Lana yet, but he'd made inquiries into adopting Georgie as his legal heir.

He'd have Georgie as a son. He had Lana as a wife. A startling, amazing wife. She had always been beautiful—she was no stranger to using that beauty for her own advantage—but tonight she had proved herself clever and strong. Despite the many challenges of Alaskan pioneer living, he had managed never to see this side of her before. How had he missed her incredible resourcefulness? Or was it that life had just beaten it out of her for a short time? Either way, Mack couldn't ignore his fascination with the woman who seemed to be unfolding new parts of her character before his very eyes. As he played blocks with Georgie and listened to her cleaning up the kitchen after Ed left, he realized that the new sheriff was not his only partner in Treasure Creek. Here he was, thinking God had asked him to take on an obligation in Lana and Georgie, when God had sent him the truest of partners instead. *Thank You, Father,* he prayed as he scooped up a yawning Georgie. He eyed the baby carriage by the door, and an idea came to him.

Plucking a blanket, his coat and Lana's shawl from their pegs by the door, he walked over to the dry sink where Lana was wiping her hands. "It's time for my walk," he said, nodding in the direction of the lavender dusk coming through the windows. "Come with me tonight."

Lana turned, her eyebrows arched in surprise. "On your walk?" Her eyes glowed in a way he felt in the pit of his stomach. "On your private evening walk?"

He felt himself grinning like an idiot, as if she'd just consented to let him carry her schoolbooks. Foolish as it was, he couldn't hope to wipe the grin from his face. She looked so immensely pleased, it just seemed to rub off on him. "Maybe privacy's overrated." He handed her the shawl as Georgie's head began to fall against his shoulder.

Lana took the shawl, growing suddenly quiet. "You pray on your walks," she said softly. "I don't think I…"

"Just walk with me. We'll figure the rest out as we go along." It had started as an impulse, but now some part of him craved her company as he walked through the town, commending its fate to the sovereign Lord who'd brought him not one but two partners today. He wanted to feel the pressure of her hand tucked into his elbow, to see the pastel sunset splash colors into her hair, to have her beside him as he prayed. He was too full of thanksgiving and satisfaction to let the sudden surge of feeling frighten him. Tonight he would allow himself to drop his endless grip of leadership's reins for a moment or two, just to see how it felt.

He helped Lana with her shawl, letting his hand linger for just a moment as he wrapped it around her tiny shoulders. He marveled at the elegant way she carried herself. A wave of affection overtook him as he slid a drowsy Georgie into the carriage and watched Lana tuck the blanket tenderly around her son. He held the door open while Lana pushed the carriage out into the gloriously light summer evening, and sighed. His evening walks were important to him, an anchor in his day, a time of worship and prayer. Was he ready to share that with his new family?

I don't know that I'm ready, he admitted to God as he pulled the cabin door shut behind them. *But who'd ever thought I'd be so willing?* He put his hand on the bar of the carriage handle and helped Lana push. "I always start down here," he said, pointing to the south side of the tiny town God had given him.

"Then we'll start down there." Lana's voice was quiet and almost reverent. He found himself wondering why it had taken him so long to invite her to walk with him. While he would have found the idea shocking yesterday, tonight it seemed the most natural thing in the world. "I won't talk—" she looked at him, her eyes melting the last of his reservations "—I won't interrupt your prayers. I'll just be beside you."

They walked in a delightful, easy silence, but she did interrupt his prayers. No matter what he prayed, no matter which house or store or family he brought before the Lord, each phrase kept ending in *"Thank You, Lord, for her."*

Chapter Eighteen

"So you'll help me?" Lucy Tucker pleaded, gripping her teacup with dirty, calloused fingers.

Lana simply could not believe her ears. Or her eyes. "Of course I'll help you," she heard herself say, although it sounded like the words were coming from somewhere other than her own body. It couldn't be real.

Lucy Tucker couldn't be sitting at her table asking her to "get done up nice" for the Midsummer Festival. This was a Tucker, after all, and Tuckers just didn't do "up nice." At least not until today. Which could only mean...

"Lucy." Lana had to choose her words carefully here, as this could be the most delicate of topics. "Am I right in suspecting there's more to this?"

Lucy straightened in her seat, but an all too feminine flush filled her tawny cheeks. "No." She might as well have nodded her head, the lie was so obvious.

Lana smoothed out the napkin next to her teacup. "It's the most natural thing in the world to want to catch someone's eye at a big party. Even for someone of your...independent spirit."

Lucy's expression softened. "Frankie'd shoot me."

Lana swallowed a laugh. "I highly doubt that. And even if she really did feel that way—" she leaned in conspiratorially "—she isn't here. It's just us." Lucy's eyes shifted left and right, her craving to share the secret warring with the shock of feminine sentiments beating inside a Tucker breast. Lana could only imagine the courage it took to come here and not only admit someone's caught her fancy, but ask for help in catching his. No wonder she'd been so easy to convince about the party the other day. "Who is the lucky fellow?" Lana whispered.

Lucy squared her shoulders and blew out a breath, bracing to shock even herself, it seemed. "Caleb."

Lana nearly knocked over her teacup. "Caleb Johnson?" The big but bookish dockmaster seemed rather mild-mannered for the likes of Lucy Tucker.

"Shh!"

"I'm sorry, Lucy, I'm just shocked, that's all."

"He's so smart. And so brave to raise poor, troubled Leo on his own. And so kind." Having sung Caleb's praises, Lucy gulped suddenly as though she'd said something wrong, as if to snatch the words back out of the air.

"No, no, I'm glad you told me. I'm just…surprised. I hadn't at all pegged you for someone so… sensitive." Still, perhaps God had matched those two well. They'd spent many hours together helping the bedraggled young men down off the trail. Now that she thought of it, they always sat near each other at town meetings. Maybe this was the real reason why Lucy spent so much time near the waterfront. Should things truly work out between them, Lana suspected only a Tucker could live up to stepmothering Leo Johnson, and Leo adored Lucy.

Poor, misguided Leo. Mack had finally located him in Skaguay, but Lana couldn't help but think it had been too late. Leo fought furiously with Caleb and Mack as they dragged him back to Treasure Creek, and things had been strained between the families ever since. More than once Lana had looked outside the church windows during school to find Leo staring darkly at the church from across the street.

Caleb deserved some happiness. And he certainly needed someone to share life's challenges with, didn't he? She made the choice right then and there to throw the full weight of her feminine wiles toward the cause of Caleb and Lucy. She'd been a skilled matchmaker back in Seattle. Why not resurrect the role out here, where families might need a little extra help to start up?

"Lana?" Genuine fear pinched Lucy's features.

Lana could not remember Lucy ever looking the least bit afraid of anything.

She clasped Lucy's rough hand in hers, black under the fingernails and all. "I'm honored you came to me. I think Caleb is a fine, fine choice for you. You have my word, I'll do all I can to fix you two up."

Lucy's face went from fear to relief, splitting in a wide grin. "I sure was hoping you'd say that. Part of me was sure you'd laugh out loud."

"Never." Lana poured more tea and began to make a mental list of all the supplies she'd need from Skaguay. Gussying up Lucy Tucker was a monumental challenge, but if she had her way, Caleb Johnson wouldn't stand a chance. "Your secret is safe with me, but there is one other person who will have to know about this in order for it to work."

"You can't tell Mack. You can't!"

Mack would howl with laughter once he knew, but Mack would not be told. No, this delicate cause must be the most private of endeavors. "Not Mack. You have my word. But we'll need Viola's help on this."

"Viola Goddard? I've barely met her. Come to think of it, most folks know next to nothing about her—except for that mysterious abandoned rich baby tale of hers."

"You know about that?"

Lucy's bawdy demeanor returned instantly. "Hon," the Oklahoma twang surging back up into her voice, "*everyone* knows about that now. Some young buck down on the docks offered Frankie fifty dollars to go coo at the baby and steal one of her moccasins so he could show up with a matching set and claim her."

A poor plan to say the least, but it proved word was out, and Mr. Brown would not be the last impostor to hound Viola's doorstep. "What did she do?"

Lucy smirked and gulped down the last of her tea. "What Frankie always does. She whipped him and took him off to Ed Parker before he could wake up."

Lana imagined Frankie Tucker huffing down the street dragging an unconscious man behind her, dumping him on Ed Parker's doorstep with a satisfied grin. Then she tried to imagine that satisfied grin under a bonnet, above an actual dress, and could only giggle. "You do have the most amazing family," she managed to say.

"Nothing truer than that!" Lucy laughed along with her.

"Now, we need to get you outfitted with some new trinkets. Do you own a handkerchief?"

Lucy produced a dusty bandana from her pocket.

"Oh my, we do have work to do." Lana went and pulled several white linen hankies from her bureau drawer. "Here are a few of mine. I'll order some hankies from Skaguay and we'll set about teaching you to embroider your initials on your own next week. Then you could think about putting Caleb's initials on a set for him as a gift."

Lucy's eyes shot wide in shock, and for the first time Lana noticed that Lucy's broad, dusty hat brim hid some very lovely eyes indeed.

Lana looked like the cat that swallowed the canary for days. She told story after story about how well things were going in the classroom, and Mack had even stolen in every once in a while just to watch her teach. When the new schoolhouse was ready, Mack found he couldn't imagine anyone else in there at the front desk other than Lana. She had a gift for teaching, plain and simple. She had a gift for organizing, too. He'd had to eat every one of his words about the load of home and school being too much for her. He'd come to realize he'd never really seen Lana for the strong woman she was. She was not the fragile flower he'd known in Seattle, nor was she the beaten-down widow he'd seen this winter. Lana was becoming another woman, a vivacious woman of strength and innovation…and an inner beauty that exceeded her stunning outer shell. He'd always found her attractive, but not especially alluring—mostly because he'd classified her as too shallow for his tastes.

He'd been wrong. There was much, much more to Lana. Life was changing the rules on him, poking holes in his carefully devised plans with fiendish efficiency, so that his precious sense of control seemed to be waning with every sunrise. It was an unnerving dichotomy: the weaker he felt, the more in control Lana seemed. Every impulse to share anything with her met an equally strong impulse to keep any shred of his inner turmoil from her view. He was her husband after all, the head of the household and charged with the protection of his family. She was becoming too precious to him to let any admissions of doubt and fear cloud her sense of security.

The nightly walks they now took together had become equally precious. He could pray over his worries with her beside him, but still not have to burden her with them. Mack found he enjoyed her company more every day. He could not only pray with her walking beside him, Mack found he prayed *best* with her walking beside him. Her uncomplicated presence—the soft hum she gave when tucking Georgie in, the way she swayed against him when they walked, the occasional glance she would give him—seemed to infuse his prayers with a sense of gratitude and praise he'd lost since the avalanche. Mack wasn't sure how he could welcome this and dread this at the same time; the war of the opposing emotions mostly rendered him speechless. He was forever grateful Lana didn't seem to mind his long gaps of silence.

Tonight, however, he could practically watch a question teeter on the tip of her control. He'd grown to know her well enough to see when she was trying to hold something in, or fearful of what she wanted to say, and it was so tonight. Lana was trying very hard not to ask him a burning question. Despite his comfort with silence, Mack was surprised to find it felt generous, not invasive, to pull it out of her. As if breaking the silence were like giving her a gift. "It's fine, you know," he said, amused at the smile he felt tugging up the corners of his mouth.

"What's fine?" Did she actually think he couldn't see the struggle on her face? How had he missed how transparent her thoughts were, back before times were so hard?

"It's fine to ask me whatever it is you want to ask."

She flushed, looking away and busying herself with a bonnet string that didn't really need adjusting. "I know you like your quiet when you walk."

"Tonight your thoughts are louder than my prayers." Mack slipped his hand beside hers on the carriage handle. "You look like you'd burst if we went two more blocks in silence."

"Was it really that bad?"

"Yes." There wasn't a hint of annoyance in his answer. Affection tickled the corners of his chest. "So—" he shrugged his shoulders "—ask away."

"What do you pray when you walk through town?"

It wasn't at all what he was expecting. Trivial questions, household purchases, town business, those sorts of questions he'd been ready for. Questions didn't come much larger than this. "Why?"

She took her time in answering. "It seems to come so easy to you. Big, formal prayers in church or tiny, friendly prayers over breakfast—they just pour out of you like they're not work at all. I don't know how you do it like that."

He'd noticed his Bible moved on several occasions, seen her listen intently over grace, watched her watching him in the pulpit Sunday mornings. He'd suspected God was, as his father put it, "shaking her soul loose" these days, but he wouldn't dare to approach her on the subject. He chose his words carefully, aware of the tender ground he now trod. "Prayers do feel like work at first, I suppose. Thinking you have to be formal and upright and all. But I've always felt God loves honest prayers best. The ones you blurt out at your worst moments, or your best moments, because you trust Him with whatever's inside you." Mack sighed, thinking that a cumbersome answer compared to the one his father would have supplied. "If that makes any sense."

He watched her turn the concept over in her mind, inspecting it. "It does make sense. Only it's not what I've ever heard in church. Well, in church in Seattle. Hymns and blaring organs and fine speeches were more like it."

"There's a place for those. I've been in some cathedrals that take your breath away, and I think they show the part of God that's awesome and mighty. He is those things, and some days we need that. Most days, though, I need God a little closer." Mack gestured at the orange sun hanging just above the blue-gray of the water. "Nature's good at showing me the God beside me. I think that's why I like it so much up here."

Lana slipped one hand into the crook of his elbow. They now pushed the carriage together, with one of each of their hands working in tandem. It felt entirely too wonderful. "Do you work it out ahead of time?" she asked. "Like your sermons?"

The thought of rehearsing his prayers made Mack laugh softly. "Maybe I should. God might appreciate it. But I don't. Mostly, I just tell Him what's on my mind, ask His guidance on things."

She rested her head against his shoulder and something slipped loose in his heart. "I think I've mostly howled complaints at God lately. He must be tired of it by now."

So she *had* prayed. A burst of gratification filled him to hear that, even if she did think it was only complaints flung heavenward. "I suspect God would rather have your honest complaints than false praises any day," he said softly, eager to encourage her. "My Pa always taught me that telling God how awful things are was the first step to making it better. Telling God your biggest problems shows you trust Him to be even bigger. At least that's what I think."

She tried that thought on for size, too, and evidently it fit, for she tucked herself in just a bit closer to him. A pair of hawks cried out overhead, their silhouettes circling each other in the darkening sky. "I never thought of it that way." She sighed. "Evidently, God must think I find Him enormous."

He had helped to set something right between her and God. The finest task a husband could accomplish. Mack made no effort to hide the broad smile he felt creep up from the darker corner of his chest. "He is."

Chapter Nineteen

Mack sat at his makeshift desk in the back of the church, frowning. He was trying to solve two problems at once: the infuriating problem of how to stretch three weeks' worth of provision stocks into six weeks' worth of store inventory, and the slightly more satisfying problem of how to get more hymnals for the growing church congregation. It seemed they'd have to start another church expansion nearly before they finished this one. A happy problem indeed.

He was making headway at neither of his tasks, and had begun pondering whether hymn lyrics would simply be written on Lana's chalkboard when Thomas Stone pushed open the church door. As the missionary to the Chilkoot Trail's many lost souls, Thomas would often visit the church when he came into town. Mack and Thomas had struck up an instant partnership, being of such like-minded goals for the region. In fact, Mack had long thought—and continued to think—that Thomas was God's choice for filling the pulpit at Treasure Creek Church. Despite his training as a preacher and having one of the strongest faiths Mack had ever seen, Stone had refused each of the times Mack shared that vision—rather like Ed. Rather like Lana. Stone lived in a crude hut on the Chilkoot Trail. If a silver star persuaded Ed, perhaps he could build Stone a real house next to the church? Mack shook his head at the thought—Lana was gaining too much influence on his tactics. Or maybe just enough. Mack put down his pencil and grinned at his own folly as Stone came straight up to the desk, gave Mack the most absurd look, and promptly emptied his pockets.

Six gold nuggets tumbled into Mack's papers in a shower of thuds Mack felt in the back of his throat.

Never, in all his scheming, did he anticipate Stone to be the one to find the decoy treasure. Mack had always believed God had a sense of humor—or at least irony—and this only proved the point. He didn't even know Stone was out looking for the gold—he didn't seem the type to chase after such things.

"I hadn't even gone looking for it," Stone pronounced, as if he'd heard Mack's thoughts. Stumped for a reply, Mack only shrugged his shoulders. "I went looking for a place to hide some provisions to take up to the trail tomorrow, and remembered the old Indian food hideaway behind the falls. Only when I reached my hand in to clear out the leaves, I felt these."

"Incredible," Mack finally choked out, still shocked. Stone found the nuggets. Nothing could have been further from his plans.

"It's nothing short of a miracle, Mack. I can't see this as anything short of a message from God. Everyone's hunting for this, I didn't even believe it existed, and yet I found it. Without trying." The missionary's eyes were alive with energy. "There isn't a clearer message of God's provision for those prospectors out there. You don't have to go out and risk your life for resources—God sends in His own good time."

As fond as Mack was of a good object lesson for a sermon, he didn't quite follow Stone's line of thinking. Nor did he think gold-hungry stampeders would see it as evidence to give up their quest for riches and await God's generous provision. Quite the opposite, they'd more likely see it as evidence of the untold riches still lurking out there for the man lucky enough to stumble upon it. The only real evidence he saw in the turn of events was that God very clearly wanted Thomas to stay in Treasure Creek. Wasn't the role of preacher the best way to make that happen? Had God just provided Stone all he needed to come down off the trail and settle into the community? Stone had told him over and over how much he loved this congregation, how it fed him to meet the challenges of his trail ministry. Now, perhaps, God was allowing him to settle into the flock he loved. The more he thought about it, the more Mack could see God's hand clearly. God was paving the way for Stone to take this pulpit.

"I can't use even half of this." Stone gathered the nuggets into two piles. He wasn't exaggerating—a single man could live as much as a year on three of those, large as they were. Stone's crude hut proved the man wasn't much for worldly possessions. "See this pile? I want to give it to the church. I want to give this church what it needs."

It needs a pastor, Mack thought. Finally, it sounded like Stone was coming to the same conclusion.

"Treasure Creek church should have the finest stained glass windows this side of Skaguay. I know you've talked about wanting them. I want this gold to pay for them."

Not exactly the response he was looking for, but Stone's love for Treasure Creek Christian Church was obvious. "That's highly generous of you, Thomas, but have you ever thought that maybe God's finally provided you the chance to build yourself a home? In town?"

Thomas blinked as if the idea had never occurred to him. "On the contrary, God's provided me for another year on the trail. Maybe two, if I'm frugal. I'd been praying for encouragement, Mack, and those prayers have been answered. Think of how many basic needs I can meet for those men up there.

Even with only the half I'm keeping, it's more than enough. And to tell those men that I didn't go looking for it, but that God provided it…can you think of a more powerful example to them?"

Mack's father would talk about the itinerant preachers that wandered through his home state— ones who would often come tired and hungry to their dinner table, but as his father put it, "on fire with the Holy Spirit." Thomas Stone's eyes shone with that same inner fire. Even as Stone went on about the needs of the men up on the trail, Mack could envision that fire igniting the faithful of Treasure Creek, a place so alive with faith that it would catch those men before they even wandered up the trail. The man was so gifted. Why did God think Stone was better used up on the trail, patching up tragedies, than down here *preventing* them?

Mack pointed to the slanted desk that served as the church's makeshift pulpit. "You could do wonders here, Thomas. Build a church home for those men. Off the trail. Help them build real lives for themselves, not just patching up troubles out on the trail. Don't you think it's time to build a home for yourself, instead of shivering in that hut of yours?"

It happened again. That shadow passed over Stone's eyes any time Mack talked of building a home. Thomas had only offered snippets of his past, bits and pieces given away in moments of unguarded conversation, but Mack was familiar enough with grief to see its scars. He knew only that Stone had lost a wife and baby, not how or when. Not that any of those details mattered in a loss so great. It was almost as if Stone was afraid to start again, afraid to put down roots for fear of losing even more. He was all too familiar with that particular dread. "Think about it, man. Maybe you've done your time up on the trail and God has new places for you to serve."

Stone just shook his head. "No. My place is up there. Now more than ever." The conviction in his eyes brooked no arguments. "But when I come down, I want to see the Sunday morning sunrise through Alaska's best church windows."

Mack tried to envision the warmth in Lana's eyes when she talked to Ed Parker. "Stone," Mack said with sincerity—more sincerity than he'd shown anyone he could remember—"I need you."

Thomas looked at him and there was a split second where Mack thought he could see some struggle in the man's eyes. As if the invitation Mack offered had some allure, but that he was denying himself such comforts. It made Mack wonder if the faith-filled man somehow thought he didn't deserve such a life. Such a contrast from the greedy consumption of stampeders he strove to serve. "Maybe," Thomas replied, pointing out to the mountain gleaming through the clear glass of the church's small window panes, "but they need me more."

* * *

Lana sat at the head of a table and wondered. How had things escalated to the point where she sat in a room full of Treasure Creek's women, holding the Gold Rush equivalent of a "beauty school"? She'd loved being known for her feminine wiles back in Seattle, to be known as the head-turning beauty with a string of suitors in tow. This felt entirely different and altogether absurd. Still, the now awakened teacher inside her took satisfaction from these women. They craved the skills she could give them. They craved all the trinkets she could give them, too. She'd handed out a dozen bows, hairpins and hankies in the last hour alone. Some of them had been in survival mode for so long they'd not given a thought to their own pampering for months. Today, she'd simply braided one woman's hair and wound it in a knot, and the room gasped at the transformation. Who knew Dinah Swanson had such a refined chin and such a lovely neck?

Would that Lucy Tucker's hair had such transforming powers. No matter how she tried to wrangle the short hair into a set of combs, Lucy's wiry locks refused any constraint whatsoever. Lana was growing frustrated, but Lucy seemed to take it in stride.

"I told you this nest has a mind of its own," Lucy lamented, tugging the comb free for the third time. "It'll never twist into anything like yours. Or Dinah's." She pointed to Mrs. Swanson, who was still posing for her flock of admirers. "You could wrestle it six ways 'til Sunday and get nowhere."

"Nonsense," Lana disputed, refusing to admit defeat. "It's just not long enough yet. We've got a while before the festival, and I've got more tricks up my sleeve."

Abby Swanson, Dinah's young daughter, walked over to Lana, wide-eyed with admiration. "Are you a princess?"

Lana remembered the time Mack's temper had boiled over after one of her whining tirades early in their journey. He had called her "a spoiled princess," and it was the truth. "No, honey—" Lana ran a hand over the girl's golden curls "—I'm Mrs. Tanner." Something happened as the words left her lips. As if the pleasure Lana had in announcing that title had come by surprise. Her mind leapt back to the time when "Mrs. Tanner" sounded like a prison sentence, the death knell for all her dreams of a future. Yet the words had just come out of her mouth with no bitterness, no resentment. No, in fact, they held pride. Instead of feeling shackled by the title Mrs. Mack Tanner, Lana realized she was, in truth, honored by it. As if she'd settled into the place she was supposed to be. The place God intended? The foreign nature of that thought, and the sheer power of it, nearly stole her breath.

"The mayor's wife, dear," Mrs. Swanson said to her daughter.

Lana felt something untangle inside, felt the

woman's words settle peacefully into her chest. *The mayor's wife*. Yes, she did like being the mayor's wife, but it wasn't from some sense of social status or accomplishment. It went much deeper than that. For the first time since coming to what she'd called "this God-forsaken place," Lana could feel Mack's vision for Treasure Creek take root in her own soul. Not a pipe dream or a money scheme, but the calling Mack so often talked about. Building lives. Crafting futures that mattered, weaving together a community. She felt it calling to her in that way Mack said God called to him.

The mayor's wife.

Mrs. Treasure Creek.

Mack's.

"How come the richest fella gets the prettiest gal?"

The question had been one yelled at Mack this afternoon by a drunk miner as he and Ed Parker broke up yet another fight on the waterfront. The docks seemed to teem with anger and blood this week. Without a town doctor, Teena Crow had been called every day, tending to injured men—half of them injured by each other. He knew enough that the drunk's question wasn't an honest inquiry—it was an accusation hurled by a down-and-out man at the unfairness of the world. Mack had endured too many bitter speeches hurled at him as he ferried the failed back home. This one had stuck in his craw all afternoon, and for all the wrong reasons; it felt too true.

Ever since his conversation with Thomas Stone about funding the church windows, Mack's sense of abundance turned strangely sour. Everywhere he turned, it seemed the world went out of its way to show him how much much more he had than others. Yes, he was a generous man, quick to help others out; but somewhere deep down he recognized an ugly hoarding instinct. A gut level greed to keep things close—mostly because he'd lost so much. Too much. Too much not to feel a niggling sense of panic at what he had to lose now. *Who* he had to lose now.

The rush of warmth he felt crossing his own threshold had begun to near choke him. Georgie's instant tackle of his knees—something that used to annoy him no end—felt like the world's purest hug. He no longer tried to hide his grin as he swooped the giggling boy up into his arms. He cared for the reckless little tornado more than he'd ever admit, even to Lana.

And Lana, well, Lana never left his mind. He worried about her, thought about her, wondered what she'd think of this idea or that project. He could barely think when he was with her, and he could think of nothing but her when they were apart. He panicked if he wasn't sure of her whereabouts and her safety—a preoccupation that bothered him beyond words.

As if to prove the drunkard's accusation right, Lana looked absolutely stunning when he walked in the front door this evening. She'd been visiting woman friends this afternoon—something fussy involving hair and dresses that he did his best to ignore—and she must have decided to gussy up for the occasion, for she looked as lovely as she had on their wedding day. She had this way of letting one curly tendril float down the side of her neck that drove him to distraction. She fairly sauntered around the kitchen this evening, which told him she was immensely pleased with herself over something— the ladies' thing must have gone well, whatever it was. When she caught his eye over a pot of something bubbling delicious scents into the air, Mack's chest did some odd jump that made him feel young and foolish and slightly out of control.

"I tell you, Treasure Creek's men are done for," she said in a sugar-coated voice that nearly made him cough. The remark struck too close to home for his comfort.

"How so?" He hoped he managed to sound gruff rather than befuddled.

"The ladies of Treasure Creek are a very pretty lot. And sweet as pie, too, most of them. We have some of the finest families in the state, you know. Or will."

There was a time when hearing Lana talk about "the finest families" would involve several inches in the social column of a city newspaper. Knowing she was talking about Treasure Creek families, however, meant a whole different thing. These were what his father would call "fine people." Lana's idea to host a town-wide celebration was a good idea, he couldn't deny it any longer. Just as he couldn't hope to deny that his wife was a truly beautiful woman. And tonight her appearance marveled any bejeweled socialite he'd met in any ballroom. "Will?"

"I expect after our little festival, many a match will be made. If you want to turn a man's attentions from gold to home and hearth, I'm here to tell you there are several very determined young ladies ready to help." She set the silverware on the table with a flourish Mack would call downright victorious. "And," she went on with a delectable smirk, "I expect some of Treasure Creek's husbands may see a side of their wives they haven't seen in far too long."

Mack fought the urge to gulp. Evidently, the richest fellows did get the prettiest wives.

Chapter Twenty

He couldn't stop staring.

All through dinner, through the mundane tasks of the household evening, Mack found himself staring at Lana. Gawking as if she were some irresistible, unfamiliar sight. He'd seen her set the table every day since their wedding, and yet tonight the curve of her wrist distracted him madly as she lay a plate at his seat. She had a delightful way of hitching up her sleeve before she opened the oven door to check if the bread crust had reached "just the right brown," or tucking a wayward curl behind the delicate curve of her ear. And yet, for all these physical details, there was something else, something undefined by shape or sound, something about her on the inside that drew him most of all. She *looked* like he *felt* when he'd set the cornerstone at the church—as though she'd settled into her place in the world and felt God's favor there. There was a spot just under his ribs that thumped at the notion that her place in the world was beside him. And that insistent thumping drummed out a disturbing message: that his compulsion to protect her had grown into something else.

If that was how a marriage ought to be, how God desired families to be, then why did the notion slip cold and icy down his spine the way it did? Was he imagining the extra warmth of her smile, the way her eyes seemed to hold on to him? Had she always smelled so distractingly unique, like flowers and spices and elegance all wrapped up at once?

"Ouch!" Lana had been trying to pull a pot from the hearth while staring at him—at least it felt like she'd been staring at him—when the potholder had slipped and left her thumb naked to the hot metal. Mack jumped up from beside Georgie and his blocks as the pot swung on its hook where she'd let it go. She winced, shaking the burned hand and sticking the finger in her mouth. "I'm such a clod," she moaned with a mouthful of finger.

The ironic image of so fine a lady yelping "clod" with a mouthful of finger made Mack laugh with unchecked affection. He motioned for Lana to come near as he pulled up the latch on the floorboard where the block of ice lay buried. Slipping the knife from his belt and a handkerchief from his pocket— handkerchiefs that now held his embroidered initials, thanks to his wife, for which he'd endured no end of jeering from workers off the docks—Mack picked off an ice chip and wrapped it for her to hold against the burn. "You're no such thing. You're the furthest thing from a clod Treasure Creek has to offer."

"Why, Mayor Tanner," Lana said, hissing as the ice hit the angry red spot on her thumb, "that was dangerously close to a compliment. I hadn't realized injury could bring out the gentleman in you."

Had she realized it was *she* that brought out the gentleman in him? Somehow, without his knowledge or consent, she'd managed to pry under the cold, driven pioneer he'd become and unearthed the gentleman he'd once been. All this time he was busy building lives, forging this ideal community out of the greedy mud that was Treasure Creek, he'd been denying himself a real life of his own.

Why? Because anything a man had or loved, a man could lose. And Mack Tanner knew that better than anyone. Thomas Stone's staunch refusal to settle down in town bothered him because it reflected his own refusal to let anyone into his life. And while he'd let—no, he'd *forced*—Lana and Georgie into his life, he'd fooled himself into thinking it was on his terms, within the limits he'd set.

Tonight, as he held Lana's hand and spread one of Teena Crow's balms on the red blister now blossoming on her thumb, Mack realized she'd gotten inside him—inside his carefully drawn limits, inside his home, inside that part of him he vowed never to let open again.

Mack had not realized, until this moment, how

much he'd wondered what Lana's hands felt like. He'd touched them before—at their wedding or in household tasks or with Georgie—but he never *held* them as he held them now. They were so much softer than he imagined, even with the rough spots work and wind had carved. Those toughened places there both bothered and impressed him. His wife's hands should be protected. His wife should know security, should never have to worry.

She looked up at him and Mack felt his heart speed in his chest. The balm was warm and fragrant, and he luxuriated in the chance to touch her hands, rubbing the balm over each palm now, not just the angry red thumb. It felt too intimate and nowhere near close enough at the same time, tangling his thoughts with a storm of emotions he wasn't ready to control.

He cared for her. He found himself second-guessing her every word like a schoolboy, scratching for any tiny proof her affection had grown to match his. Then again, as he looked in her eyes it seemed impossible that she didn't feel what he felt. Her neck was flushed, her breath came in the short gulps of intensity he felt in his own chest, and Mack realized if he had half the courage folks attributed to him, he would kiss her this very second. Halt the silly pretense and cross the line they'd so neatly drawn across their relationship. Be a true husband to her, not just a guardian or protector. She deserved no less. But the gulf between them was so wide and full of grief, Mack wasn't sure it could ever be crossed.

Instead of kissing her, Mack chose something far more daring. For the first time since Jed's descent into desperation, Mack Tanner was going to let someone else in on his plan.

"Lana," he began unsteadily, "I've been thinking."

"Have you now? About what?" She was still close, still looking up at him with huge, doelike eyes.

"I'm done with all this hiding and scheming. I'm going to take all the gold and go back to what I know. Oil and land. No more gold. Land is what no man can take away from me. What no one could take from you or Georgie, either."

Her eyes widened. "Land? You mean you'd leave Treasure Creek?" She said the name as if it was home to her, as if leaving—the very thing she'd once begged Jed for months to do—were an awful thought.

"No, dear." The endearment slipped out of his mouth, surprising them both. "Treasure Creek will always be home. But there is a tract of land north of here that's rich in oil. Oil is what will hold the future here, not gold. I can't keep those fools from seeking my gold, but they'll have to stop once they know the gold is gone. It's the thing that will stop all this, getting rid of the gold by using it—all of it—to buy land. Land is security, Lana. For us. For you and

Georgie and even Georgie's children. For…" he felt something give way inside when he used the words "…for our family." He couldn't look at her at that moment, focusing instead on the salve he worked into her hands. She had the most delicate, elegant hands; and now that he held them he couldn't stop touching them, working the salve all over each hand now, rather than just over the small wound. "It's too dangerous these days." He hated the way his voice caught, but the words clawed their way out of him, demanding to be spoken even as he tightened his grip on her tiny hands. "I need to know they'll stop bothering you. I need to know you both will be provided for no matter what happens, and only land can do that."

Her eyes glistened. "We're fine, Georgie and I."

"No, you're not. You're a walking target, and I'd go out of my head if anything…" He couldn't finish the sentence. Couldn't admit what he was coming to feel, what drove him to tell her his plan when he'd kept so much to himself for so long.

"I'm fine," she repeated in a whisper that near undid him. Silently, she wrapped her hands around his instead of the other way around, so that she held his hands. Looking down at those hands, he seemed to watch from miles away as she raised his hands to her lips and placed a tender kiss on the back of each hand. So tender an act from this spitfire of a woman. "Gold or no gold, I'm fine." The touch of her lips felt like the softest thing in the whole world against the weathered skin of his hand, bursting through him like the heaving cracks of the melting ice flows he'd seen in the bay. A tiny fissure that spread unchecked until even the largest of ice walls fell to its gap.

"Lana." The single word surged from him, as rough and uncontrolled as the tearing open he felt in his chest. He'd told her his plan, and instead of feeling awful and exposed, he felt a strange, spacious freedom that was both exhilarating and downright terrifying. As if the wide open crack in his chest wouldn't kill him after all. Before he could stop himself, Mack leaned down and kissed her. A cautious, small kiss that wasn't small at all, but rather enormous and powerful, lasting years instead of half a second.

When he opened his eyes, Mack felt as if he'd just bolted out onto a wildly rickety bridge, swinging in the middle of the huge gap between them, unsure whether to keep going to the other side or lunge back.

Lana stared at her husband, stunned. She hadn't planned this. She had wanted a nice evening, a special meal, and even to look her best, but she had fooled herself into believing it was just a shallow indulgence. Each small pleasure she saw in Mack's eyes, each cautious smile or lingered gaze had slowly unwound her intentions until the evening had become far more about pleasing Mack than about pleasing herself. He'd jumped in with that overprotective manner of his when she'd foolishly burned her thumb, but instead of annoying her, the strength of his reaction touched something raw in her. She felt things in his fingers, things she had caught fleeting glimpses of in his eyes, things she discounted and doubted and wasn't sure she even wanted. She knew his hands to be rough and strong, yet they tended to her with unspeakable care.

More than that, Mack had shared his plan with her. She knew how much that cost him, what a step that was for him to take. She did not hate this man. She had never hated him, only chose him as the target for her widespread resentment at how the world had turned for her. His slow, steady care suddenly seemed infinitely stronger than any wild declarations of love Jed had ever made. Stalwart. Trustworthy. A man whose affections, once given, would never be taken away. No, the world had not turned against her, she was coming to see that now. Slowly, through the view of the faith Mack was tugging out of her, Lana had begun to see each bend in her journey as connected segments, as a path laid out by a wiser hand. She could believe, feeling Mack's calloused fingers make circles in her palms, feeling the catch of his breath and the glow his words produced in her heart, that perhaps God had not abandoned her at all. That He'd perhaps given her someone new to love.

The kiss was small. Timid, even, and yet it thundered through the both of them as though the house itself shook on its foundations. His wide eyes told her Mack was no more sure of his feelings than she, that neither of them knew how to go from here. This was not a moment for sweeping romantic embraces—things were far too delicate for that. She knew, in that moment of mutual panic, that their relationship would grow in inches, in tiny but trustworthy steps. And she surprised herself by being glad of it.

Still, Mack looked as if he might fall over any second if she did not make some sort of response to his kiss. Smiling, filled with a tenderness that she quite honestly thought she couldn't feel ever again for a man, Lana pulled up one of Mack's strong hands. She laid her cheek against the tanned back of his palm, eyes falling closed at how warm and strong it felt. These were hands that would protect her, defend her, and now perhaps, love her. He smelled of smoke and spice and the strange balm that still made her hands tingle. A split-second jolt of astonishment shot through Mack's fingers as she heard him suck in his breath. A cautious, shocked delight played in his eyes and he grinned, clutching her hands.

Pressing, unfortunately, right onto the large blister now grown on her thumb. Her yelp of pain broke the spell of the moment. Mack jumped and flipped over her hand, ever the protector, to inspect the wound.

"Still hurts?" he said unsteadily. His composure had indeed suffered as much as hers in the last minute. "Teena Crow's balm usually works faster than that."

Alarmed, Lana pulled her hands from his. The tingling in her hands now felt unwelcome and strange. How had she not noticed the markings on the clay jar? She'd never had been able to trust their odd practices. She'd heard too many stories—both here and from her father in Seattle—of illnesses made worse by native potions. When her papa was sick, Lana's mother had once caught one of the staff doing strange things to Papa in the name of "healing." Papa had died shortly afterward. Mama fired the native maid in such a torrent of accusations that Lana had never been able to override her deep mistrust of native people as healers. "What was it?"

Mack's eyebrows furrowed as he stepped back. "It's a Tlingit healing salve from Teena Crow. It will help."

He hadn't asked. He'd just put it on her. He was always doing things without asking. Lana's thumb throbbed. Now both hands had a disturbing prickling sensation that wouldn't stop, even as she fussed at them with a dishtowel. She hated the thought of crude potions on her skin. The potion frightened her. His use of it, even though she'd admitted to him that she didn't like Indian medicine, bothered her even more. Telling herself she was overreacting, Lana scrubbed her hands with the towel as she made for the sink, but instead of helping, it tore open the blister. Now the concoction stung sharply, even as the strange tingling increased. "Why did you use that on me? You know I don't..." She found she couldn't finish her sentence without sounding horribly judgmental, but that's exactly how she felt. She'd been afraid of the native Indians she'd known in Seattle and many she'd met here and in Skaguay. "Don't put their potions on me. Ever."

"Lana, it's just a balm." His look only made her feel angrier about her reaction. "It's not even medicine."

"How could you just go ahead and use something like that when you know how I feel about it?" Lana washed her hands twice, but the oily nature of the balm wouldn't leave her skin, nor would the infernal tingling. "It won't stop stinging. It won't come off." The pain fed a panic she didn't want.

"Don't be silly. You know Teena. She'd never harm you." He tried to grab her hand but Lana spun from his grasp.

"Don't call me silly. Is that what you think I am? Is it silly to want to know whatever's in that concoction you used on me?"

Mack's frustration lowered his tone. "I have no idea what's in it. But I've used it for years and it works. I know you distrust Tlingit medicine, but this is just a balm. A harmless lotion. You've got no reason to act like this."

So he felt she was some kind of fool for mistrusting Tlingit medicine. And as her husband, he was going to set her straight by simply overriding any opinions he didn't share? Suddenly this became about much more than a simple burn on her thumb.

As if he'd heard her thoughts, Mack let out an exasperated breath. "Lana, this is foolishness. The Tlingit are good people. I've used salves like that for years. I'd never give you anything that would hurt you."

He'd stopped just short of saying "trust me," and she knew why. How many times had they toed up to this argument over trust, dancing around the corners of it, never really coming out and accusing each other of mistrust? Why now, when he'd just taken what she knew to be a huge step of trust toward her, did this roar up between them? He might never deliberately hurt her, but it was clear now he'd not learned to respect her opinion. Or to trust the value of her thoughts if they differed from his. He'd decided what to do about "Mr. Brown" and Nicky Peacock. Leo had stolen from her, but it was Mack who decided to ship him upriver to some horrible fate in a Skaguay jail. All the faults in their relationship suddenly lay wide open before her. The warmth that had filled the room moments ago was gone, replaced with the icy silence of the answer she didn't give Mack.

He felt it, too. "Fine," he barked out, flinging his hands into the air. "Be unreasonable." His words had sharp edges—the ruined moment had stung him as deeply as it did her. Why were they so skilled at hurting each other? Why did their every attempt to grow closer end in frustrated pain? *Father God,* Lana prayed, as she twisted the dishtowel between her stinging fingers, *this can't be what You wanted for us.*

As if in reply, a churning rumble of thunder came from the bay. The storm that had threatened all afternoon was finally showing its face. *Perfect timing,* she thought bitterly. "You're going out?" Lana raising her eyebrows in surprise when Mack pulled his hat and coat off the pegs by the door.

"It's a bit cool in here for me."

How had they let a tiny disappointment escalate into this? "Mack…"

"I was planning to go dig up that gold tonight anyhow." He pulled the coat on, and the set of his shoulders told her he'd planned to do it under her blessing, not like this.

"But the storm…" It wasn't what she really meant to say.

"It will only help matters. Darker and all." Raindrops began their splatter as a flash of distant lightning lit up the water streaks on the windowpanes.

Lana regretted everything and yet knew nothing had really changed. They were hopeless with each other. She wanted to yank the evening back to the glowing moment when Mack took her hands and she began to believe they might stop hurting each other. She wanted to tell him not to go but couldn't find the words.

His eyes told her there was no stopping him anyhow. Whether or not it was wise for both of them to cool off apart, he was going. He settled his hat on his head with such resolute firmness that any final plea died in her throat. "Be careful," she managed, but the words sounded choked and hollow.

"I'm *always* careful," he replied after he turned toward the door. He stopped with his hand on the latch but didn't look up. "I thought you knew that."

The words echoed in the room long after the door's harsh slam.

Chapter Twenty-One

Mack turned his head down into the wind and kept walking. *Who was that woman I saw tonight?* He'd seen sides of Lana he'd never seen before—both good and bad. And glory, what had possessed him to kiss her? Even if he thought of her like that—and it surprised him how much he *had* begun to think of Lana like that—it was a fool thing to do. When did he become such an impulsive dunce? Still, when she raised her eyes under those thick lashes and looked at him, her hands all soft and warm in his, he felt like twelve kinds of fool. Ready to grasp the impossible notion that they might actually have *that* kind of marriage. After all that stood between them, how could he ever think that possible?

And yet he had thought it, had felt it, which made her next reaction so hard to swallow. Lana? Afraid of the Tlingit? Sure there were lots of folks who weren't quick to trust the natives, but he'd never counted Lana among them. It had been a split-second's impulse to heal her wound. How had it turned into an argument about forcing his opinion on her? *I've married a stranger,* he admitted to himself—and maybe even to God—as he turned his collar up against the strengthening storm. Someone I don't know. Or never knew.

But someone he'd promised to protect. To honor and cherish, even if she confused the daylights out of him at the moment. It seemed wrong to go back on that plan now, even though he couldn't really say why. He just knew trudging up the muddy trail seemed somehow a less foolhardy path than going back to that confounded woman right now. Muttering to himself, Mack pressed on through the weather with his pack and shovel slung over one shoulder until he found himself in the spot off the trail where he'd hidden his gold.

It felt good to dig, even if he was soaked as he worked. The exertion of unearthing the gold seemed to burn through his frustration, give him a safe place to put the anger he'd nursed all the way up the mountainside. It must have taken the better part of an hour, but it only felt like minutes before he heard the clink of his shovel against the tin box. "Ha!" he said, raising his face to the storm in defiance of no one in particular. Mack squatted down, cleared the mud from around the four corners of the box, and had begun to lift it when something came out of the dark and knocked him back hard, sending him headlong into the hole he'd just dug and wrenching his shoulder.

He scrambled out of the hole, yelling, when the form came at him again, this time wielding the shovel Mack had just used. "Who the...*umph!*" Mack nearly toppled back into the hole as he blocked the shovel's arc toward his head. Whoever it was meant for him to fall into that hole and not get out.

"Here?" a voice with a southern twang called out as he brought the shovel around again. "In the middle of the trail? You're more idiot that I thought, Tanner."

That makes two of us, Mack thought, scrambling back out of the hole and reaching for the gun at his belt. He'd been so lost in his anger at Lana he'd never once looked up to see if anyone was following him. He was just pulling his gun from its holster when he heard the click of the other man's gun. A flash of lightning revealed Nicky Peacock behind a silver pistol aimed at Mack's head. What were his last words to Lana? "I'm always careful"? Mack said a quick prayer that those really wouldn't be his *last* words to Lana and slowly lowered his gun to the ground. "Easy, Peacock. Let's nobody get hurt out here."

"Won't nobody get hurt long as you do what I say, Mr. Mayor." The young man aimed the shiny new gun between Mack's eyes. "Now, you just hoist that hefty box outta its hiding place nice and slow."

He didn't have a choice. As slowly as he dared, his mind scrambling for options that wouldn't come, Mack began pulling the heavy box from its muddy surroundings. Rain and sweat drenched him as he lugged the box onto the grass, the wind whipping wet hair into his eyes and the rain sluicing nearly horizontally through the trees. Peacock, slight as he was, was having enough trouble staying balanced in the fierce, wet wind, and Mack found himself wondering how soaked Nicky's pistol could get before it would cease to fire. That could work in his favor, but the large and equally new knife that hung from the man's belt could do damage no matter how wet it got. Mack's own knife was out of reach, tucked in the pack now slumped at the base of a nearby tree. "You followed me." Mack couldn't think of anything else to say as he wiped his muddy hands on the grass.

Nicky cocked his head to one side. "Been in town for days. The way you been buyin' pretty things for Lana, I figured you'd need to get more gold sooner or later. We all know you don't do business with Jameson—or any other bank—don't we?"

He'd snuck back into town without Mack knowing? He'd been watching Lana? A new chill—one that had nothing to do with rain—ran down Mack's spine. "Don't trust bankers—and your pal Jameson least of all." The longer he kept Peacock talking, the more time it bought him to think his way out of this.

"Do you trust your pretty little wife, Mr. Treasure Creek?" Even in the darkness, Nicky's toothy grin gleamed in a way that made Mack's skin crawl.

"What's that got to do with anything?" Mack disliked the question. Intensely.

Peacock brandished his gun. "More than you'd think. Ever stop to consider it ain't your charm that won the little lady, but what you got hidden up here? Ladies like your wife like to be well kept, don't they?"

"Don't even mention my wife!" Mack didn't bother to keep the snarl from his voice.

"You just open that there box and leave the missus to me." He cocked the pistol hammer again for emphasis. "She gets half, she'll be fine."

Stunned, Mack surged forward at the insinuation, but the man leveled the gun straight at his forehead. Mack flexed his fingers, with only the barrel of the gun keeping his simmering rage in check. Had he been anywhere but two feet below the arrogant cad, with his own boots stuck in mud, Mack would have attacked by now. Peacock would be lucky if Mack left him alive to be jailed for attempted robbery. As it was, he could only pretend to fiddle with the box lock as he tried to find a way onto level ground. "You lie. Lana doesn't even know you."

"Am I lying?" Smirking, the man dug into his coat pocket and produced a handkerchief. Mack recognized it instantly as Lana's, the purple embroidery edging had been one she'd chosen during their wedding shopping trip in Skaguay. "We go back a long ways, Lana and I."

She'd said she recognized him down on the docks that day, Mack recalled. Had that first "attack" been a ruse? A setup for now? No. He wouldn't let himself believe such a thing.

Mack hurled the box into Peacock's knees with enough force to knock him over. He kicked the man's gun out of his hand and the pair of them rolled along the wet ground, each going for the large knife at Peacock's belt. Peacock got to it first, slicing a sizable gash in Mack's forehead that blurred his vision with blood and rainwater. They grappled for what seemed forever, splashes and grunts filling the soaked night as they banged into trees and rocks, wounding each other. Just when Mack thought he had the upper hand, Peacock picked up Mack's gun that had lain on the ground. With a victorious grin, he pulled back the hammer with one hand while moving the knife he no longer needed down back toward its sheath. Desperate, Mack lunged one last time, hoping to get the gun before it went off. As he tackled Peacock by the waist, pushing the arm with the knife away, they backed up over the box of gold and went down together. The gun fired at his side, and for a moment Mack was unsure if the burning he felt was just the heat of the barrel or the bullet's path through his gut.

Mack fell in a heap on top of Peacock, a sharp pain searing his other side as well. For a moment

Mack thought he'd been both shot and stabbed, until underneath him Nicky jerked violently and let out a grotesque gurgle. Mack pulled himself off the convulsing body to see the bloody tip of Peacock's knife coming through the back of the man's coat. Nicky Peacock had fallen on his own blade, and it had gone straight through his chest to nick Mack in the ribs. The gun, still warm and smoking, lay a few inches away. Grasping his stomach, Mack exhaled to find only a small stream of blood from the knife and a powder burn on his shirt. The gun had fired beside him, not into him. He sank back on his haunches, shocked and grateful to be alive.

He stared in disbelief at the handkerchief now lying soaked and smeared in the mud beside them. It was Lana's. Peacock had one of Lana's handkerchiefs, one purchased by the very gold he sought to steal. Could Lana really have been in league with Nicky Peacock? It seemed impossible, but Lana never left her handkerchiefs anywhere. She was especially careful with them. Stolen? No, Peacock would have stolen something valuable like jewelry, not handkerchiefs. If they were partners, and Mack gasped at the thought, it did explain something that had bothered him for weeks. Why she was nowhere near as unsettled at that first "attack" down on the docks as a lady of her nature ought to be.

Had he been foolish to think a lady of Lana's nature would ever really want to make a home in a place like Treasure Creek? Mack wiped his hands down his face, only to realize he was still bleeding. He pressed the guilty white handkerchief to his forehead, smelling her soap in the linen, even as he tasted blood. Every man eyed Lana. Every man eyed his gold. Was it such a far cry to think she'd eyed his gold, too? Yes. No. Possibly. Lana knew how to partner up with folks to gain an outcome. She always craved attention. Mack sat down on a rock and pondered if his own wife had conspired to rob him. Maybe hurting him hadn't been in the plan. Still, if she'd somehow worked out how to follow him to where he hid the gold—and she was smart enough that she might have—it would be easy as pie to convince some greedy fool to seize his chance.

Peacock lay still on the ground, his face half in a puddle that was blooming a stain of red, as blood trickled from the his mouth. Blood but no breath. Nicky Peacock was dead.

Mack staggered a bit, the weight of what had just happened settling on him like lead. Everything he'd feared, everything he'd worked so hard to prevent, had just exploded into reality in front of him. He tried to tell himself he knew better, but his suspicious nature could not be tamped down.

Fear and anger fed each other quickly, and any attempts to shore up his temper were lost within minutes. He'd been a fool to trust anyone. God gave him a clever mind to protect Treasure Creek, and he'd let Lana's mesmerizing eyes lead him into foolishness. "Wise as serpents?" He'd been anything but. Growling from anger as much from the effort, Mack pulled Peacock's body off the trail. He'd have to deal with Peacock's body later. He'd made arrangements in Skaguay that couldn't wait. The gold was out of its hiding place and there was no telling who Nicky Peacock had bragged to or conspired with. It was tonight or not at all.

Mack didn't even bother to undo the lock, but smashed it open with the butt of his gun. He piled the gold into the knapsack he'd brought for just that purpose, groaning under its weight. The many pokes of gold dust and lumpy nuggets made for an awkward, painful load, digging into his back and shoulders, even as the rain still stung his face. None of that compared to the cavern in his chest where he felt the sting of Lana's betrayal. It nearly crushed what breath he had left. He'd stop back at the cabin to let her know she hadn't succeeded in fleecing him, then he'd go to Skaguay and buy the land where he would move. Settle on the farthest corner of the land and watch Treasure Creek scheme and connive itself into the doom he tried so hard to prevent.

It had been hours. Lana was certain something was wrong. Mack had been angry when he left, but even his temper wouldn't lead him to do something foolish on a brutal night like this. Nor would he leave Georgie and her alone all night—even in his worst moods—without telling her. *Dear Lord,* she prayed, *something is wrong. Something has happened to him. I can feel it. Help me!*

The fragile bit of security she'd allowed herself to feel shattered at the possibility that she and Georgie could be alone again. She had fooled herself into thinking God had any loving plans for her…the future held nothing but endless pain and heartbreak. Not only for her, but for Georgie. It was as if she watched her life dissolve as uselessly as the garden dirt melted into Alaska's ever-present mud.

Even if Mack was all right, their marriage was far from fine. Had he never really seen her as worthy of his confidence? Had she only imagined the closeness growing between them? It hurt to consider that his feelings for her weren't anything more than dry obligation. Just another facet of his role as Ideal Family Man and Mr. Treasure Creek.

Family. She had thought they'd built the first beginnings of a new family. She looked at her beloved son, his eyelids drooping as he slumped in Mack's stuffed chair by the fire, blissfully unaware of the storm going on outside—and inside—their home. The unfairness of everything—the unending avalanche of disappointment—drowned her in more pain than she thought any soul could survive.

Just as she thought every tear was shed, as she tucked a blanket around Georgie who—worst of all—had sighed, "where's Ugle Ack?" as his head hit the pillow, Lana heard the cabin door latch click open.

Lana hurled into the main room. "Where have you been?"

"You know exactly where I've been."

That was the very heart of it, wasn't it? She *didn't* know exactly. "No, Mack, I don't know where you've been, because *you would never tell me.*" He'd lied about going after the gold, anyway, for he had nothing with him—no gold, no pack, no shovel— nothing but the rain-soaked clothes he left in and the coat he refused to even take off.

He pointed at her, his eyes as dark as when he'd thrust his shovel against the necks of those young robbers. "And wouldn't you be eager to know my secrets? Have at my gold? Is that the only thing you ever really wanted from me? You like all the gifts I bought you well enough, but I supposed some appetites can't be satisfied."

"What are you talking about? I told you I didn't want your gold." Truth, trust—*those* had been what she wanted from him, not the land or gold or security he thought was the currency of his world. If he couldn't see that after all this time, he never would.

Mack stalked across the rug. He turned from her, planting his hands on the fireplace mantel with a fierce thud. "I would have given you anything you wanted. But it's never enough. I always wondered what drove Jed to the lengths he went for fortune, but maybe I understand now. It doesn't matter whether it was earned or stolen, begged or borrowed for you, does it? Just as long as there's more." He turned to her, and the dark despair made his eyes look so deep and hollow her breath caught in her throat.

Lana was stunned by his accusation; it seemed to come out of nowhere. "What are you talking about? What have I ever done to make you think like this?"

"Demanded my secrets."

"Expected your trust," she corrected. Georgie began to cry at their raised voices. She moved toward the door to Georgie's room, suddenly wanting to be nowhere near Mack and his rage.

He followed her. "You schemed behind my back. You betrayed me." As he turned, she noticed one side of his shirt held a large red stain. And he had smears of blood and dirt all over his pants.

"What happened to you?" She picked Georgie up and sidled past Mack to take her son into the main room again, the air was much too close in here.

Mack didn't follow her at first, but after a moment the sudden quiet clung to the house with suffocating power.

He came out of their room, holding her jewelry box. He slammed it on the table so hard one hinge pulled out of the wood. "I'll tell you what happened to me. Nick Peacock, that's what." He reached into his back pocket, and the size of the red stain on his shirt almost made Lana gasp. She did gasp when he clenched one of her handkerchiefs in his fist.

"Where did that come from?"

"Nicky Peacock. He followed me upon the trail tonight. Really, Lana, I suppose it's a compliment to you that I was too bamboozled by your earlier performance to look over my shoulder."

"What's Nicky Peacock got to do with anything? Why were you up on the trail tonight?"

"You know why!"

"No, Mack, I don't. You told me you were going to get the gold, but who knows what you were really doing? I see no gold. Why are you hurt? What happened?"

Mack held his hands out in an empty gesture. "You're right. I don't have the gold. I'm lucky to be alive, so I'll be thankful for that, I suppose. If you're so determined to get your hands on the great Tanner fortune, you've had what you need all along, Lana. I've told you where the map is."

"You've never really showed me the map, Mack. You don't trust me enough to show me, do you? Even if you dug it up this moment, I know that map isn't enough to find the gold. It was all too clear you couldn't trust me with the whole truth. You trust no one. No one."

"The map has a key." He pointed to the jewelry box. "Your pin. Take the pin you love so much and go dig it up yourself, for all I care. I'd just as soon never lay eyes on you again. Poor Georgie. It's not *his* fault that neither his mother *nor his father* could be trusted." With a growl she felt to the bottom of her shoes, Mack threw the handkerchief on the table.

He reached into his coat pocket and withdrew the map. The one he'd told her was buried in the garden. Had he dug it up tonight, or had that been another of his deceptions? "Keep whatever you find. Peacock planned to keep your half of the gold anyway. You'll have to rip the initials out of the handkerchief, though. This marriage is over and you're on your own again." For the second time tonight the cabin door slammed shut with enough force to shake the house.

His mistrust felt like a physical blow. Had they really learned so little about each other in this brief, odd marriage? Why on earth would God call him to marry her, as he had asserted again and again, only to put them through this pain? Even as she paced the room, her eye drew back again and again to the stained handkerchief, the folded map and the now-splintered jewelry box, as if they were symbols of her ruined life. What kind of man would believe the word of a thief like Nicky Peacock over that of his wife? She'd never given him any reason to think she'd scheme with the likes of Peacock to rob him of his gold. Even with Jed's many deceptions, Lana couldn't recall a man so quick to mistrust, so sure the world was nipping at his heels. Everyone thought so highly of Mr. Treasure Creek, but even through her anger Lana could see he was a collection of deep wounds held together by sinews of faith.

Georgie had quieted, and the growing silence allowed Lana's anger to melt into a deeper fear.

Mack wasn't himself. The man she saw behind those horrible dark eyes wasn't really her husband. She was hurt and angry, that was true, but as she stared at the blood that stained her handkerchief and thought of the size of the cut on his head and the red blotch on his shirt, she realized how none of this made any sense. Something was very, very wrong here. The fear gripped her more tightly, as if the isolation of the cabin would swallow her alive.

Lana grabbed her coat and Georgie's, pulling his tiny trousers on under his nightshirt. "We're going to the Aunties, honey. We need their help." Yes, it meant revealing one of Mack's precious secrets, but too much was wrong to worry about that now. She couldn't hope to sort this out on her own; her mounting dread was already clouding her thoughts.

"Cookie," Georgie exclaimed with a smile, despite his tears.

"Yes, cookie. Help and cookie." Lana made sure to close the door without a slam.

Chapter Twenty-Two

Telling the story seemed to make it worse. Lana fought back tears too many times as she recounted the night's drama to the Tucker sisters and Caleb Johnson. Lucy had convinced everyone to go over to Caleb's house, since, as dockmaster, Caleb would know if Mack indeed had left for Skaguay as he said. There was no ferry this late at night, but Mack had many friends who might transport him as a favor.

Leo seemed especially disturbed by Lana's story. "You're sad. And mad. That's wrong," Leo said with a growl in his voice. "Mr. Mack is a mean man."

"He's an angry man, that's for sure," Caleb replied, taking off his spectacles and pinching the bridge of his nose. It was so late it was early, the stormy night slipping into a dull grey dawn long before sunrise ever showed in Seattle. "And clever," he added, raising one eyebrow at Lana. "Who would have thought he made the map key in the pin he gave you?"

"And why not tell me!" Lana shot back, more confused than ever. So many layers. He trusted her with the pin but not with its purpose. With the map but not with the key. She regretted revealing Mack's secrets, but something had to be done and she needed to decide what. Had she just betrayed the growing closeness she'd imagined between them, or had it never been there at all? Her heart couldn't believe the events of the last few hours. Mack. Nicky Peacock. Lana's heart tumbled over and over in her chest, a storm of hurt and anger, and a growing fear that the Mack she knew had been a lie. Or had gotten lost.

"It's nothing we'll sort out tonight," Caleb concluded with a yawn. "Best let everyone simmer down 'til morning. We'd best hope things look clearer in the light of day." With a tiny joy she couldn't feel for herself, Lana noticed Caleb take Lucy's hand for a moment as they said goodbye. There really was something between those two. She wanted to feel pleasure at the tender surprise of it, but couldn't muster the energy to feel anything but hollow loss. She could only hug Georgie tighter as he slept on her shoulder, ignoring the weak "it'll all work out" comments Lucy offered as they walked home to her empty house.

Sleep was impossible. While Georgie was fast asleep in his room, ignorant of his new family's unraveling, Lana sat staring at the barest remains of a fire in the hearth. Not knowing what else to do, she'd pulled aside the movable brick in the fireplace where she'd stuffed the map before going to Lucy. There were so many things in that hiding place! With a gasp she unfolded notes from a lawyer in Skaguay—Mack had looked into the process of adopting Georgie as his own son! And there were rough sketches of a larger house, a big home with room for a large family. Lana couldn't reconcile the man of these papers with the bitter, angry soul who had stomped out into the storm tonight. Again, the suffocating sense of everything going wrong twisted around her throat. She had to find him. Desperately, Lana stared at the map, trying to work out how Mack's pin served as a key. No matter what she did, the map remained a confusing puzzle of lines and curves.

Not too much later, there came a rap on the cabin door. Mack would hardly knock, but then again, Mack was doing things she couldn't hope to understand tonight. Lana rushed to the door, only to discover Leo standing there.

"Leo?" His face bore none of the childlike affection she usually saw in his large brown eyes. The darkness she saw in its place sent ice down the back of her neck.

"Get that pin," he said in a voice that didn't even seem to belong to him. "I heard you talking at Papa's house. I'll show Mr. Mack how smart I am."

"Leo, I…"

Leo produced an enormous knife. "Get it!"

If only she'd put the jewelry box back in Georgie's room, maybe she could climb out the window and run for help. But Leo had already seen the map and the pins laid out on the table. "We can't leave. Wait until morning."

"I heard you say the pin you love most. Get it. We're going to get the gold now."

Lana backed up toward the table. "I don't know where the gold is, Leo. I don't know how the map works. I can't help you find it."

Leo raised the knife. "You think I'm not smart enough to make it work? That's all anyone thinks, isn't it? I'm smart enough to steal, I am. You'll all see." He seemed twice his huge size, filling the room with a dangerous anger.

Georgie's only chance at safety was to stay asleep in his room. He'd been up most of the night, and Lucy had promised to come by first thing in the morning. It seemed a horrible option, but Leo looked capable of anything, and if she couldn't save herself, she could save Georgie. *Oh, dear Lord above, save him! Save me!* She cried the prayer in her heart as she took Mack's pin and laid it out before Leo on the table. *Mack,* her heart moaned as Leo began moving the pin around on the map, lining it up this way and that, *what's happened and where are you?* Lana tried twice to move away from the table, to inch toward the door, but each time Leo would look up with burning eyes and point to a chair. How many times had she told him to "sit back down" in school? Leo was at war with his world and everyone who'd dismissed him—Mack included, it seemed. Bent on revenge with a dangerous determination. She could only hope to keep him calm enough to head off before Georgie woke up.

"Got it." It took Leo all of ten minutes to fold the map up in such a way as it showed a design clearly matching the brooch. How strangely dull and keen that man-child's mind worked, that he could unlock a puzzle that stumped her but still not see the foolishness of what he was doing.

"Everyone will know you took the gold, Leo. This won't work. You'll be in worse trouble than before. Stop this and we'll talk more."

"No!" Leo growled loudly. "Everyone will know. Everyone." He wasn't making sense, wasn't connecting that everyone knowing would be the doom of his plan. "We're going now."

"You've got the pin and the map, you don't need me, Leo." Lana used the light and encouraging voice that had charmed him in the classroom. "You've worked it out on your own, you're smart enough to do this without me."

"No, you're coming. *Now.*" He scooped up the pin and the map in his huge hands and motioned toward the door with his knife. A light rain had started up again, she could hear it against the windows. She'd probably be lying dead in the Alaskan mud somewhere before the end of the day. *Oh Georgie, to leave you an orphan. Would God be so cruel?*

Lana had no idea how long she and Leo trudged through the cold dawn, following whatever clues Leo had uncovered from the map. One minute she thought he'd worked it out, the next minute they'd take some odd turn and she'd hear him grind his teeth in frustration. Once or twice she tried to talk him into giving up his search, but it only darkened his mood, and the more angry he got the less clearly he seemed able to think. *Lord, I'm done for,* she cried silently, sure she would not survive the day. Leo seemed ready to turn on her any minute, sure she was withholding the secret of Mack's gold no matter how she tried to convince him otherwise. Looking into Leo's twisted features, Lana recalled Mack's words: greed made men animals.

"Stop that!" Leo yelled at the unfolded the map, for the steady rain would smear the markings further every time he opened it to reposition the pin. She could only hope, as the land sloped upward, that they were somewhere near the Chilkoot Trail and its steady stream of stampeders, where someone might come to her aid. "Stop it! Stop it!" he yelled at the clouds, his rage now fully unleashed. He threw the map on the ground and stomped it into the mud, taking an enormous rock and throwing it on top. Bellowing, he threw the pin in the mud as well, and Lana scrambled after it. This was the wrong thing to do, for the last thing Lana remembered was the shadow of Leo's enormous hand coming down over her face with a force that sent sparks flying through her vision.

"Mr. Tanner! Mr. Tanner!"

Mack raised his head off the desk in his hotel room. He'd waited outside the land grant office where he'd arranged to be the first transaction of the day. He didn't sleep until he'd disposed of the wicked gold and held the land deed in his hands. If it were up to him, he'd never see an ounce of gold again.

He'd gained his land, but lost everything in the process. The empty hole in his own chest screamed out what he'd refused to believe: he loved Lana and lost her. He had done what he'd sworn never to do, left himself open to the pain of losing someone close to him. Again. Early this morning, as he held the land deed that was to be his future, all Mack could think was that it was impossible to know which hurt worst—to be betrayed again or to have his heart crushed again.

Another set of pounding on the hotel room door. "Mr. Tanner!" It was Jimmy Crow's voice. Teena Crow's brother.

Mack yanked open the door to see a haggard looking Jimmy with his hand raised to pound yet again. "You must come now. Your wife is ill. She hit her head hard up on the trail and Teena is very worried."

Mack's heart twisted into a pinching knot. He didn't need to ask what Lana was doing up on the trail. Some part of him wanted so badly to be wrong, to discover that she did somehow love him, but he'd been blinded by Lana's charms and Georgie's innocence.

Georgie.

"Is Georgie all right?"

Jimmy looked puzzled. "The boy? He is not with you?"

Fear shot down Mack's spine. Even if she were twice the deceiver he thought her, she would never leave Georgie behind. Not even for all his gold. "He most certainly is not. Has anyone checked the house?"

"I went by on my way to you. It's empty. And torn up. Things toppled over, tossed everywhere." He lowered his voice and raised one eyebrow. "Did you fight?"

Mack's stomach gave a lurch. Did the people of Treasure Creek think him capable of violence in his own home? "Of course not!" Mack shot back, grabbing his coat and hat. "Well, we had an argument, but not like that. Have you got a fast horse?" If he took the Tlingit trail back and rode hard, he could make it there faster than any ferry he could hire.

"Bolt is the fastest horse in the village. It is why I brought him to you."

Reaching into his coat pocket, Mack threw the poke of gold dust he'd kept onto the table. "This should more than cover your ferry ride home. You have my thanks, Jimmy."

Jimmy smiled. "Just remember you have my horse."

Mack battled with himself the entire ride, worry for Lana and Georgie warring with confusion over what had really happened last night. The hour ride pounding through the back trail had pummeled one sure truth into his brain: he'd been foolish. He'd allowed his wounded, suspicious nature to jump on Nicky Peacock's accusations about Lana *with no real proof.* Worse yet, he'd not even been man enough to confront Lana directly with the whole of the matter. He, who preached and strived to help Treasure Creek stay clear of Alaska's rampant deception, had fallen prey to it easier than a tenderfoot stampeder. He'd believed Nicky Peacock over the woman he cared most about. Believed a deceiver's story over what his heart knew to be true, and paid the price for his foolishness. Mack was too easily convinced he had lost Lana because he'd allowed himself to love her. Fear spawned as many sins as greed; perhaps more. While he'd always thought himself a visionary, he wasn't. He was just a foolish, frightened man undone by his own obsession to be master of his fate. To manufacture his own future instead of trusting that future to God.

It was full daylight by the time Mack turned Bolt into the clearing outside of the town that held the

Tlingit village. If God granted him the chance to set things right with Lana, he'd move heaven and earth to do so. He just hoped he hadn't come to his senses too late. "Teena Crow!" he called into the village, barely waiting for Bolt to skid to a stop before throwing himself off the horse and heading for Teena's dwelling at a full run.

He nearly tackled the healing woman as she ducked out of the entrance. "Peace, Mack. She is resting."

Mack grabbed the small woman's shoulders. "Is she all right?"

"Thank God Leo did not do worse. Leo is a big man and the knife could have done her great harm."

"Leo?" Mack had steered clear of Leo expressly to let things simmer down. Had that angered the young man? More importantly, had Leo become enraged enough to take it out on Lana? "Leo stabbed Lana?" The words seemed too horrible to even speak. He tried to push his way past Teena into the dwelling, but the feisty healer held her ground, planting her small hand squarely on his chest with glowering eyes. "It was a small cut, not meant to kill. It will heal with the balm I've put on it. But her head worries me more. Thomas and several others were up by the waterfall and found Lana farther down the trail. She was lying near several large rocks, and she has a gash behind one ear where I am sure her head struck one of them."

The thought of Lana lying unconscious and bleeding up on the Chilkoot was enough to shred Mack's chest from the inside. He could barely breathe, and yet he seethed with anger at the same time. He'd sworn never to kill in vengeance, but… "So help me, if I find Leo Johnson I'll…"

"Leo is long gone, Mack. I fear he is lost to us. I fear he was lost to us long before this. Do not let your heart wander down that path. Your heart is needed here. Lana is asking for you. And Georgie."

In his desperation to get to Lana he'd nearly forgotten no one knew Georgie's whereabouts. "Georgie…" he moaned, pulling his hands down his face and pacing the ground. He'd failed as a husband, a father, a protector.

"Georgie is a smart boy. God's hand kept him safe, Mack."

Mack spun to look at Teena, air finally finding its way into his lungs. "He's safe?"

"Georgie hid from Leo under the bed. Lucy went to your home once Thomas told us Georgie was not with Lana. And thank the Lord he wasn't. Georgie is safe. Frightened, but safe. The Tuckers are keeping him for now. Lana must rest."

Right now the most important thing in the entire world was to get to Lana and see her open her eyes. To ask her forgiveness for believing what he never should have believed, to beg her to allow him the chance to restore her trust. He squared himself at the Tlingit woman, pulling himself up to his full height over her tiny frame. "I must see her. Now."

She looked at him for a long moment, eyebrows knit together as if examining his face. "I had to be sure your heart was right before you saw her. But I see that it is. You may see her."

Mack made to duck past her into the tent. Again the tiny hand shot out to block his way.

"Say only what is most important. Everything else can wait until she is stronger, can it not?"

Even in the shadows of the room, Mack treasured every detail of Lana's features. Her hair was down and mussed, her neckline ripped on one side, and he could see where Teena had tried to clean off the mud and blood as best she could. He thought of her lying alone and injured in the rain, and regret stabbed his chest. What a sorry pair he and Lana made. They had done such a miserable job with each other, deepening wounds God had meant them to heal. *Redeem us, Father,* Mack prayed as he took Lana's hand. He could still see the blister from where she had burned herself last night. He also saw the shiny coating on Lana's thumb where Teena had dressed the blister again, reapplying the healing salve onto the red raw edges of the wound where Lana had tried so hard to scrub it off. *We have both made such a mess of the healing You meant to do. I beg You, grant me a future with her,* he prayed. The strength of his affection for Lana—his *love* for Lana—swelled up inside with a power he didn't know how to control or contain. *My plans have only led to pain. When did I forget to seek Your plans? Give me a life with her, Lord, a future with her and Georgie. Only, grant me a new heart with it. The change is too big to do on my own.*

Lana stirred, opening her eyes with a wince of pain. "Easy there, love, go slow." He brushed a lock of hair from her forehead. "You've a nasty bump."

"Mack?"

"I'm here." The lump in his throat choked any further words.

She began to rise. "Georgie…"

"Is safe. Lucy Tucker has him. Your son was smart enough to hide from Leo but knew to come out of hiding for a Tucker cookie."

"Oh, Mack, you were right about Leo. I thought he would kill me for the gold. He got so fearsome when he couldn't make your pin work the map."

"My pin?"

"Well, of course, your pin. You told me the pin I loved the most would work the map."

His pin. In his jealous rage, he had yelled at her to take the pin she loved most. And she had taken his pin, not Jed's. He'd turned those brooches into some kind of test, forcing her to choose between him and Jed. That was so far beyond wrong, and all his scheming had made his pin a trap instead of the gift it should have been. Lana had selected his pin, even when she should never have been forced to choose. She did love him. *Heaven above,* Mack lamented, feeling his heart break, *I have been the king of fools.* "The pin I gave you doesn't work the map, Lana. Jed's pin does."

"But you told me to use the pin I loved the most…" Her eyes brimmed over. "And you thought that was Jed's pin. You just couldn't see I'd come to care for you, could you?" Her smile was sad. "And I've been terrible at showing you, haven't I?" She sighed and brought her hand to rest atop his. "At first I wouldn't wear it, that's true, but then I couldn't bear not to keep it safe. I didn't want it bent up like Jed's. It's such a beautiful thing. And now it's ruined."

"I don't care," Mack said fiercely. "You're safe." He shook his head. "I should never have believed Nicky Peacock when he said you were in league with him. I was too hurt to see how impossible that was. I'm sorry I suspected you when I should have trusted you most. With everything."

"We hurt each other, Mack. But I don't want either of us to hurt anymore. You were right about so many things. About Leo. About the danger. About Teena. If the Tlingit hadn't found me…"

He put a finger over her frown. "Don't. You were right. I've never trusted you. Not completely, even when you earned it. I told myself I'd never lose another partner after I lost Jed. After *we* lost Jed. I thought I could outsmart every danger on my own."

She moved to rise further, and Mack held her by the shoulders to help her upright. She seemed at once all too frail and amazingly strong. She narrowed one eye at him. "You're a very smart man, Mack Tanner, and I expect you could do every job in Treasure Creek. But there's one even you can't do."

I love her. It seemed as clear as day, as close as breath, as if his heart had known it all along, but it only just reached his thick head it this very second. "What's that?" he said, feeling a broad smile spill over his face.

"You can't be God. You can't master the future anymore than you can master people. Believe it or not, you taught me that."

"How can I teach you something I don't seem to know?" She reached a hand up to cup his cheek, and he felt the stubble of his unshaven chin prickle her tender palms. Glory, but she was a wonder. The perfect woman for him. How could he have ever thought her an obligation? Lana was a gift. "I've been such a stiff-necked idiot."

"Every teacher knows the best way to fully learn a subject is to teach it to someone else. And we've both been terrific fools, Mack. But I'm ready for things to change. I think God has a wonderful future laid out for us, fortune or no. And I don't think we have to be wealthy or crafty and clever to get it. We never had. We've just had to be faithful." She reached up with her other hand, so that she held his face in her hands. "And honest. And to be honest, I love you. I think I'd been too hurt to really see it before. But I see it now. The night we kissed…"

"The night we fought because I…"

She stopped her words with a hand to his mouth, and the touch washed through him, a torrent of grace. "Shh. I see it clearly now. I love you and I love our family. I thought God cruel to force us together, but now I think Him wise beyond anything I could dream."

God was, in fact, wise beyond anything Mack had ever given Him credit for. "I love you. I was just too afraid of losing you to let myself admit it. When I think of what all my conniving might have cost me…" Mack pulled her up onto his lap with incredible ease, wrapping his hands around her delicate waist and feeling as though God had crafted her uniquely to fit in the circle of his arms. In the darkest corners of his heart. "How did I miss that my real treasure is you?"

She didn't bother to answer. Only let him kiss her like the wondrous, precious treasure that she was. As she wrapped his hands around his neck and kissed him back, Mack felt his heart break open and change into the new one he'd asked of God only moments before.

Chapter Twenty-Three

Lana spent the next hour convincing both Mack and Teena—who put up a unified opposition to the notion—that she was perfectly fine and able to return to Treasure Creek. Her head throbbed, but her heart would continue to throb much worse until she held Georgie safe and sound in her arms. Finally, the pair of them relented, but only when she threatened to walk back on her own, with or without their consent.

Wearing the enormous smile that had not left his face since their reunion, Mack set Lana gently in Bolt's saddle and swung up to settle in behind her. Lana had lived in Treasure Creek for almost five months, yet it felt as if she were entering the town for the first time. The clarity of the summer sun, the blinding green lushness of trees and grasses, the gleam of the snowcaps that never left the mountains; she took all these in with a new vibrancy. As if she saw her place in the world with new eyes. She leaned back into the warmth and strength of Mack's chest, and it struck her that despite all that had happened, she actually felt safe. *Thank You, Lord,* she prayed, feeling the words chime in her heart like a bell. *I haven't felt really safe in so very long.*

She must have sighed, for Mack tipped his head down to look at her. "Are you all right?"

"Yes, really." She meant it in ways she never had before. "I'm just glad to be home."

She felt a chuckle tumble through his chest. "Teena walks this path every day. You were never far from home."

Lana turned to look at him, even though it made her neck twinge to do so. "No, it's more than that. Lying in the forest, I hollered at God for all He'd taken from me. I was hurt and angry for not getting the life I'd wanted. The splendid life my parents always made me feel was my birthright—you know, fine things, grand adventures, influence in high places."

Mack stared at her, puzzled by the words. "Those things aren't up here. It always did make me wonder why you came here with Jed in the first place."

"I came to find the shortcut to the fine life. Don't you see, Mack? I realized I wasn't much better than those foolish men up on the trail. Hunting for something I think will make me happy, when in reality it's not the thing that will make me happy at all. Even if Leo had pulled up the gold and handed it to me, I wouldn't have wanted it."

"It wasn't there anyhow, Lana. I meant what I said when I told you I was digging it up to buy land. To build a big new house someday for our family. I thought by taking the gold away I could protect you better. Instead, I left you in danger." She felt his breath catch at the thought.

"But you were right about the gold. In some ways, Mack, I *did* want it. But only because I believed that lie that it would secure my future. Only it's just that—a lie. More trap than treasure, because the life I thought it would buy me—well, it isn't what I really wanted after all." She let herself snuggle in against him. "Listen to me, I must sound silly."

"Lana Bristow Tanner preaching that money doesn't buy happiness? You did take a large knock to the noggin."

She grinned. "Don't you stop buying me pretty things. I never said I didn't still like them."

"Oh no?"

"Well, I know *now* they're not what makes life work." She slid a hand onto Mack's sleeve, running it down the muscles of his arm until it rested atop his the back of his hand. "God's given me other treasures. I don't want a big fancy home outside of town, Mack. I have my home—and the life I really want, here with you and Georgie in Treasure Creek."

Mack twined his arms tightly about her and kissed the top of her head. "Does that mean I can cancel that order of china from Seattle?"

"Absolutely not. In fact, we might need to double it."

"Double it?"

"Just because I know what's really important in life doesn't mean Mr. and Mrs. Treasure Creek won't keep a full social calendar. You can add on to a house just as easily as you add on to a church, you know."

Mack moaned. "I thought Teena told you to rest for at least a week."

"She did, but you're forgetting the Midsummer Festival is only two weeks away. I have no intention of postponing, so you'll have to help. I take it the General Store's ready to open on schedule?"

Mack blew out an exasperated breath. "Anything but. And the renovations to the church are a full three weeks behind. It'll take an act of God to keep things on plan."

"Maybe that's exactly as it should be."

For the next two weeks, dozens of Treasure Creek residents pitched in on the school construction while Mack did double duty supervising a huge crew of workers finalizing the General Store. Treasure Creek had never seen anything like it, and Lana couldn't have been more proud. Once the saw blades arrived from Seattle, the little log church would grow in size and gain siding, a real steeple and other improvements. Treasure Creek was fast on its way to becoming a real town, not just a settlement sprouting up at the root of the Chilkoot.

Finally, tonight Treasure Creek's First Annual Midsummer Festival was at hand.

Everyone was decked out in his or her finest, gathered around a collection of tables in the church yard. Lanterns and ribbons hung from the tree branches, blue and white-checkered tablecloths fluttered, and all kinds of food sent spectacular scents wafting through the evening breeze. The MacDougal plaid did indeed make its appearance. The biggest surprise of the night, however, was the Tucker sisters. It took a full ten minutes for anyone to recognize them. Viola Goddard had managed to make them dresses that suited each of their king-size personalities perfectly. Mack nearly gasped when he figured out who they were, making Lana laugh out loud. "Hang me," he muttered, his gaze shifting back and forth between the trio and his grinning wife. "There really are ladies under those Tuckers!"

Mack's gaze was only exceeded by Caleb Johnson's, whose mouth actually fell open when Lucy strolled—and gracious, she did indeed *stroll*—by him. No one ever did see Leo again, which left a mile-wide hole in Caleb's heart. Lana suspected God had plans to heal that wound—plans that just walked by in an unexpected swish of calico. "Mack," Lana said with a sad smile, "Treasure Creek needs a preacher now."

"I've been trying to convince Thomas Stone for

weeks, but he won't budge." Mack glanced down at her, his eyebrows lowering suspiciously. "Why?"

Lana pointed over to Caleb, who was currently bent over Lucy Tucker's hand, kissing it. "I give it three weeks. Two if I'm persistent."

He crossed his arms across his chest. "Good thing I asked Margie to watch Georgie for the night, not Lucy. She looks a mite preoccupied. I don't know, though, Lana, Tuckers don't marry."

Lana jutted her chin at her husband. "Tuckers don't marry *yet*. Caleb deserves some happiness after all he's been through. And what do you mean Margie's watching Georgie tonight?"

Mack laughed and pulled on her arm. "Oh, I've one final scheme up my sleeve. But I promise this is one you'll like." Tugging her to a shady corner on the other side of the church, he pulled out a small velvet pouch. "While I've no intention of stopping the purchase of pretty things for my wife, I decided tonight would be a good time to start over."

She didn't know quite what that meant, but when she pulled the drawstring on the little pouch, a beautiful jeweled gold cross emerged. Set with, she realized after a moment, the stones that had been in both brooches.

"I had them both melted and made into this. Don't hide it in your jewelry box, Lana. I want to see it around your neck every single day."

"I'll never take it off. Oh, Mack, it's so beautiful. And perfect." She turned so he could fasten the clasp, luxuriating in the kiss he planted at the base of her neck once he did so.

"There's more." He had the oddest look on his face as he reached into his coat pocket. "I've written a little something."

Lana's hand flew to her chest. "A love letter? Mack, you outdo yourself."

He actually flushed. "Not exactly. But I suppose you're close. Read this."

He held out two pieces of paper. One was the deed to a large parcel of land just north of Treasure Creek—the one he'd gone off to purchase the night everything had gone wrong. Only Mack's name had been crossed off the document, replaced by "Whomever Holds This Deed." The other was a small folded note. Lana angled it toward the patches of lavender light still left by the evening sun and read:

"This map should be used to find the buried treasure only in dire times. Dire times brought the contents of this box to you. This is your treasure. In the finding. In the hoping, in the faith.
Yours, Mack Tanner."

Lana looked up at him. "But, Mack, that means anyone could claim that property."

"That's right. Anyone. You or Georgie. Our children or our grandchildren. Anyone. I figure God has someone perfect in mind at the perfect time."

Lana was stunned. "So you're leaving it up to Him, are you?"

The pastel light caught a distinct gleam in his eye. "Well, I intend to help a bit on the children and grandchildren part." He pointed to the church where a blanket, lantern and small basket of goodies lay stashed. "After the party, we're going treasure-hiding tonight. Just you and I. Together. That way you'll always know where to find it if you need it. No secrets. No schemes…except the one giving you and me a whole lot of time to treasure ourselves."

Lana felt her whole body warm to the idea of an entire night completely alone with her husband under the canopy of Alaska's stars. God had given her true love, dear friends, a splendid family and the adventure of His perfect plan for her life. She smiled and touched the cross before wrapping her arms around Mack to thank him good and proper. "Treasure, indeed," she whispered into his neck. "But the Mayor shouldn't leave his own party early."

Mack grinned. "Says who? As far as I'm concerned, it's the perfect distraction. They'll all be too busy celebrating to come look for us."

Hand in hand like youngsters, Mack and Lana grabbed supplies and were just about to set off toward the trail when a young boy broke into the clearing. "Mr. Mayor, you gotta come now."

"No, I don't," Mack nearly growled.

"Oh, but you do. There's two big men got into a big argument over the blueberry pie. They says you have to decide. And there's some other man asking about some golden baby?"

"Tell Mr. Parker to take care of it."

"I tried." The boy pointed back in the direction of the growing ruckus. "He's too busy fighting with one of them Tucker sisters."

Mack's grip on Lana's hand tightened defensively. "Which one?"

"I dunno. Never could tell them apart. And now they got dresses on besides, so I'm not even really sure they are Tuckers. Mama says she rightly expects to see a pig fly tomorrow, but I can't figure out what she means by that."

"Teena Crow!" Margie's voice shouted from somewhere behind Mack. "You better get on over here and patch this fella up before he bleeds all over my new dress. Frankie hit him something fierce."

Mack growled and raised a hand to dismiss the boy when Lana tugged his arm. "Go do your duty, Mr. Mayor, I'll wait. It's sunset until midnight around here anyway. That's just one of the blessings of living in Alaska.

* * * * *

*Don't miss the next novel in the
ALASKAN BRIDES series.*
Klondike Medicine Woman *by Linda Ford
is available where
Love Inspired Historicals are sold.*

Dear Reader,

Treasures. We seek them in one place, only to find them in the last place we thought to look. The world sees treasure as something you can hoard, but the wisest among us see the lie in this. God ignores a man's possessions but values his soul, ignores a woman's beauty but treasures her compassion. Why then, do we so often run after something that only *looks* like success or security? We try to engineer our own fortunes, but that is God's domain. He loves us and wants only the best for us—even when it takes us far too long to figure that out. I hope Lana's and Mack's story helps you recognize the true treasures in your own life. As always, I love to hear from you at www.alliepleiter.com or P.O. Box 7026 Villa Park, IL 60181.

QUESTIONS FOR DISCUSSION

1. Do you think Lana had other options than to marry Mack? What would you have done in her place?

2. "Get-rich-quick" schemes have been around for centuries. Where's the "gold rush" these days? What are its dangers, and how can we protect ourselves?

3. Have you had an idea catch hold of you like Lana's idea to teach did? Did you act on it? Why or why not?

4. Do you have a daily ritual like Mack's evening walk? If you don't, what like that might appeal to you?

5. Georgie brings out an element of Mack's personality that's been gone for too long. When has a child brightened your life? Why are they so good at it?

6. How would you have felt if you received a pin like the one Mack gave Lana? Why was it or wasn't it a good idea? Was he right or wrong to use it the way he did?

7. Is the "six-nugget treasure" a wise tactic or a lie? Why?

8. Mack says, "People were always believing things in spite of the hard truth in front of them." When has that happened to you? What opened your eyes to the truth?

9. Have events ever made you angry at God like Lana was? What's the best thing to do with those emotions? If you're not pleased with how you handled that season of your life, what can you change in the future?

10. Would you have been as harsh on Leo as Mack was? Why or why not?

11. Have you ever seen "the words of scripture pierce a heart"? Felt it yourself? What was the result of such a powerful experience?

12. If you had found the gold nuggets like Thomas Stone, what would you have done with them?

13. Do prayers come easy to you like they did to Mack? Or do you feel uncomfortable with praying like Lana did? If you're not happy with your prayer life, what can you do to change it?

14. What's the role of honesty in a marriage? Are there secrets worth keeping, or are all secrets kept from a spouse dangerous?

15. Have circumstances ever kept you from trusting someone you should have? How can we fight such deceptions? How do we fix mistakes of mistrust?

INSPIRATIONAL

Inspirational romances to warm your heart & soul.

Love Inspired

HISTORICAL

TITLES AVAILABLE NEXT MONTH

Available May 10, 2011

KLONDIKE MEDICINE WOMAN
Alaskan Brides
Linda Ford

HANNAH'S JOURNEY
Amish Brides of Celery Fields
Anna Schmidt

ROCKY MOUNTAIN PROPOSAL
Pamela Nissen

THE UNEXPECTED BRIDE
Debra Ullrick

LIHCNM0411

REQUEST YOUR FREE BOOKS!

2 FREE INSPIRATIONAL NOVELS
PLUS 2
FREE
MYSTERY GIFTS

Love Inspired

HISTORICAL
INSPIRATIONAL HISTORICAL ROMANCE

YES! Please send me 2 FREE Love Inspired® Historical novels and my 2 FREE mystery gifts (gifts are worth about $10). After receiving them, if I don't wish to receive any more books, I can return the shipping statement marked "cancel". If I don't cancel, I will receive 4 brand-new novels every month and be billed just $4.24 per book in the U.S. or $4.74 per book in Canada. That's a saving of at least 23% off the cover price. It's quite a bargain! Shipping and handling is just 50¢ per book in the U.S. and 75¢ per book in Canada.* I understand that accepting the 2 free books and gifts places me under no obligation to buy anything. I can always return a shipment and cancel at any time. Even if I never buy another book, the two free books and gifts are mine to keep forever.

102/302 IDN FDCH

Name _____ (PLEASE PRINT) _____

Address _____ Apt. # _____

City _____ State/Prov. _____ Zip/Postal Code _____

Signature (if under 18, a parent or guardian must sign) _____

Mail to the **Reader Service:**
IN U.S.A.: P.O. Box 1867, Buffalo, NY 14240-1867
IN CANADA: P.O. Box 609, Fort Erie, Ontario L2A 5X3

Not valid for current subscribers to Love Inspired Historical books.

Want to try two free books from another series?
Call 1-800-873-8635 or visit www.ReaderService.com.

* Terms and prices subject to change without notice. Prices do not include applicable taxes. Sales tax applicable in N.Y. Canadian residents will be charged applicable taxes. Offer not valid in Quebec. This offer is limited to one order per household. All orders subject to credit approval. Credit or debit balances in a customer's account(s) may be offset by any other outstanding balance owed by or to the customer. Please allow 4 to 6 weeks for delivery. Offer available while quantities last.

Your Privacy—The Reader Service is committed to protecting your privacy. Our Privacy Policy is available online at www.ReaderService.com or upon request from the Reader Service.

We make a portion of our mailing list available to reputable third parties that offer products we believe may interest you. If you prefer that we not exchange your name with third parties, or if you wish to clarify or modify your communication preferences, please visit us at www.ReaderService.com/consumerschoice or write to us at Reader Service Preference Service, P.O. Box 9062, Buffalo, NY 14269. Include your complete name and address.

LIHI1

Amish widow Hannah Goodloe's son has run away,
and to find him, she needs help—which circus owner
Levi Harmon can provide. If Hannah can convince him.
Read on for a sneak preview of HANNAH'S JOURNEY
by Anna Schmidt, the first book in the
AMISH BRIDES OF CELERY FIELDS *series.*

"I HAVE REASON TO BELIEVE that my son is on your train," Hannah said. "I have come here to ask that you stop that train until Caleb can be found."

"Mrs. Goodloe, I am sympathetic to your situation, but surely you can understand that I cannot disrupt an entire schedule because you think your son…"

"He is on that train, sir," she repeated. She produced a lined piece of paper from the pocket of her apron and handed it to him. In a large childish script, the note read:

Ma, Don't worry. I'm fine and I know this is all a part of God's plan the way you always said. I'll write once I get settled and I'll send you half my wages by way of general delivery. Please don't cry, okay? It's all going to be all right. Love, Caleb

"There's not one word here that indicates…"

"He plans to send me part of his wages, Mr. Harmon. That means he plans to get a job. When we were on the circus grounds yesterday, I took note of a posted advertisement for a stable worker. My son has been around horses his entire life."

"And on that slimmest of evidence, you have assumed that your son is on the circus train that left town last night?"

She nodded. She waited.

"Mrs. Goodloe, please be reasonable. I have a business to run, several hundred employees who depend upon me, not to mention the hundreds of customers waiting along the way because they have purchased tickets for a performance tonight or tomorrow or the following day."

She said nothing but kept her eyes focused squarely on him.

"I am leaving at seven this evening for my home and summer headquarters in Wisconsin. Tomorrow, I will meet up with the circus train and make the remainder of the journey with them. If your boy is on that train, I will find him."

"Thank you," she said. "You are a good man, Mr. Harmon."

"There's one thing more, Mrs. Goodloe."

Anything, her eyes exclaimed.

"I expect you to come with me."

Don't miss HANNAH'S JOURNEY by Anna Schmidt, available May 2011 from Love Inspired Historical.

Love Inspired HISTORICAL

Save $1.00 when you purchase
2 or more Love Inspired® Historical books.

SAVE
$1.00 when you purchase 2 or more
Love Inspired® Historical books.

Coupon expires September 30, 2011. Redeemable at participating retail outlets in the
U.S. and Canada only. Limit one coupon per customer.

52609783

Canadian Retailers: Harlequin Enterprises Limited will pay the face value of
this coupon plus 10.25¢ if submitted by customer for this specified product only.
Any other use constitutes fraud. Coupon is nonassignable. Void if taxed, prohibited
or restricted by law. Consumer must pay any government taxes. Void if copied.
Nielsen Clearing House ("NCH") customers submit coupons and proof of sales to:
Harlequin Enterprises Limited, P.O. Box 3000, Saint John, NB E2L 4L3, Canada.
Non-NCH retailer: for reimbursement submit coupons and proof of sales directly
to Harlequin Enterprises Limited, Retail Marketing Department, 225 Duncan Mill
Rd., Don Mills, ON M3B 3K9, Canada. Limit one coupon per purchase. Valid in
Canada only.

U.S. Retailers: Harlequin Enterprises
Limited will pay the face value of this
coupon plus 8¢ if submitted by customer for
this specified product only. Any other use
constitutes fraud. Coupon is nonassignable.
Void if taxed, prohibited or restricted by
law. Consumer must pay any government
taxes. Void if copied. For reimbursement
submit coupons and proof of sales directly
to: Harlequin Enterprises Limited, P.O. Box
880478, El Paso, TX 88588-0478, U.S.A.
Cash value 1/100 cents. Limit one coupon per
purchase. Valid in the U.S. only.

5 65373 00076 2   (8100)0 11736

LIHCOUPON1